The House on R. Street

The
House
on
R. Street

A NOVEL BY

Sheila Kohler

Alfred A. Knopf   NEW YORK   *1994*

Library of Congress Cataloging-in-Publication Data

Kohler, Sheila.
 The house on R. Street / by Sheila Kohler.
  p.   cm.
  ISBN 0-679-42606-X
 PR9369.3.K64H68   1994
 823—dc20   93-20720
                       CIP
Manufactured in the United States of America
First Edition

For the "real" Bill (1908–1983)
and, again, with gratitude to
Gordon Lish, my teacher

And to the mother as she falls asleep
And as they say good-night, good-night. Upstairs
The windows will be lighted, not the rooms.

—*Wallace Stevens*

Spring

Look at her.

In the early afternoon, when the sun is at its height, she slips down the carpeted steps, passes through the hall with its dusty proteas and shell-shaped cups and saucers locked in the china cabinet, opens the door, and steps forth into the light. She stands for a moment, shadowless. She looks at the placid blooms of the jacaranda. She runs through the garden, past the seringa tree, past the red-hot pokers, past the hibiscus. She skates her hand across the top of the box hedge. The spring sun is as sultry as at the height of summer. She runs in the shade of the driveway under the oaks, past the agapanthi that sparkle silver-blue in the shadows. She runs through the white gate, swung open between white gateposts. She runs alone through the light along the street. She catches the tram on R. Street in the early afternoon, in the dead time of day.

She leaves the house after luncheon. The family—Mother, Father, Uncle, and the three children—sit around the mahogany dining table, with the shutters closed on the light and the flies. The furniture is dark and ugly and smells of cloves. A thin bronze clock ticks loudly against the green wall. Embroidered doilies cover the arms of the chairs, and there is a ginger jar on the mantelpiece.

The luncheon of breaded pork chops and roast potatoes and gem squash from the garden, of steamed pudding and stewed apricots with custard is passed around by a blind servant in silence. Sometimes the servant puts sugar instead of salt in the soup. He scratches at the swing door, shuffles in with the steaming serving dishes. His toes stick out from the sides of his sand shoes.

Look. The family staggers from the table. The sisters, Dorothy and Hazel, who study domestic science, return to their embroidery. The mother retires to the sickroom for her rest. The father stares at stones in a shaft of mote-flecked light. The uncle retreats to the shadows of the back bedroom.

. . .

Cicadas.

A bird dives down low and then flares up high in the white sky. A black victoria passes, and Bill hears the clippedy-clop of the horse's hooves as she runs to catch the tram. She rides the tram that goes past the house on R. Street. She runs down the street in her school uniform, her white blouse missing the top button open at the neck, her panama hat anchored onto the back of her head by the thick elastic under her chin.

In the afternoon, the garden is very still. The mother lies down with a migraine. The father dozes over diamonds. Dorothy and Hazel knit and whisper, their dark heads close, their voices murmurous with the sound of boys' names. The blind servant sits on his haunches with his back to the brick wall in the courtyard in the sun and smokes his pipe.

As she runs for the tram, Bill smells the sun on the hard dry earth and the smoke from the servants' coal fire in the courtyard. She smells the pigs. Even the pigs stop grunting and snuffing in the heat of the afternoons. Haze says, "They're so quiet because they know John's going to kill one before supper."

After luncheon, she is supposed to be at school, but she does not care for it. Sometimes she stays away from school even in the mornings. She climbs trees, or she plays football with the boys, or she gambles for stones with the nanny's twins under the mulberry tree in dark sand.

She has trouble with numbers. When she tries to hold on to them, they slip through her fingers. Once, at school, she is found with the carving knife in her satchel. "Let me see what you have got there. Are you listening to me, Bill? I said, let me see what you have in your satchel!" Miss Sparks, the headmistress, demands when she catches Bill with the carving knife in her satchel. "What on earth are you doing with a carving knife at school?" Miss Sparks exclaims. When she says an *S* she whistles.

"It's to sharpen my pencils," Bill retorts, and looks the headmistress in the eye. Her gaze makes the headmistress pull on the black hair that grows from a wart on her chin.

In the early mornings, Bill stands at the window with her palms pressed against warm glass and makes her mother step forth into the garden. In the gold light, her mother shines. Bill makes her mother's eyes shimmer blue-green and her skin glow and her hands drift smoothly through the air. Bill makes her mother float in tranquil brightness across the lawn while the blind servant pushes the mower across the grass. Bill brings her mother forth together with the dew on the grass, the sunlight in the leaves, the blue breast of the sky, the abundance of the world around her: green lawns, mauve jacarandas, and golden oaks, the flowers, the red hibiscus that grows by the window, the fat blue hydrangeas, the plumbago under the palms, the orchard of nectarine, peach, and plum, the vegetable garden, the rose garden, and the pink-gray veld that stretches out to the distant hills.

Bill's mother always calls Bill Little Pet or Angel and allows her to do exactly as she likes. Her father plays Chopin waltzes for her in the evenings on the upright piano. The nanny's twins do what she tells them to do. Her sisters, mostly, do, too. Uncle Charles always says, "Bob's your uncle" when she asks him to do anything for her. Even when Bill was very young, even when they called her "fat white woman," she would look them in the eye, and they would run.

Her favorite game is Simple Simon. She jumps up and down on the lawn and flaps her arms and shouts, "Simple Simon says do this, do this, do this, do that." When she says "do that," she changes the position. Her sisters, the eldest, called Dottie, the long, thin one with the sallow complexion and the dark hair on the upper lip, and the youngest, called Haze, who is plump and pink and white, sweat in the heat and the sun. They flap their arms. They jump up and down. They turn puce. They echo, "Simple Simon says do this, do this, do that."

When Bill refuses to drink her milk, Haze does, too. Bill's mother looks at Haze. Her mother shakes her head and says, "You would put your head in the fire if Bill did, wouldn't you?"

. . .

Bill sits beside Hazel on the tapestried piano bench before the upright piano in the lounge with the faded curtains drawn on the fierce sun. Hazel throws her limp plait behind her shoulders and caresses the keys. She plays a measure of a Mozart sonata and plumps her foot down hard on the damper pedal. Her mother says, "Hazel's the musical one."

Dottie stands beside them with her big hands folded on her flat chest and flutes in a thin voice. Her favorite is "Cherry Ripe," but sometimes she does, " 'Early one morning just as the sun was rising, I heard a maiden singing in the valley below,' " pressing her hands together hard, her voice taking on pathetic tones for the refrain: " '*Oh*, don't deceive me, *oh*, never leave me, *how* could you treat a poor maiden *sooo*.' "

Bill lets her shoulders slump, kicks at the piano leg, and sticks her tongue into the side of her cheek. Her mother says, "Now, girls, don't leave my Little Pet out."

Hazel strikes the keys superiorly with plump hands. When Bill touches the keys, the notes sound separate, angular, like something hard and sharp. They jangle, and Hazel makes the sign for an organ grinder. Every time Bill plays the wrong note, Hazel lifts her gaze to the ceiling. She thrusts forth her bottom lip. Bill keeps playing the wrong note. Hazel keeps saying, "For goodness sake, try to *concentrate*, will you?"

Once Hazel slams the piano lid down on Bill's hands and bruises them. There is a raw mark the color of a strawberry along the backs of Bill's hands, and she re-treats to Uncle Charles's room at the back of the house.

She is about to catch the tram outside the redbrick house with the corrugated iron roof and the walled garden. Because of the roof, the house is torrid in summer and freezing in winter. The walls of the house are thin. You can hear a whisper anywhere. The floors shake when you walk across the parquet.

It is that dead time of day when the women shut them-selves up in their rooms for their rests or play languid scales on their pianofortes or ply their needles in the shade of the laburnum tree. It is the time of day when the servants sit outside at trestle tables and eat mealie meal. The servants drink mugs of sweet milk tea or stretch out in the thick grass beside the road, their hats tipped over their eyes. The men nod off at their desks in their small, musty offices. The only sound is the shrilling of the cicadas. At first, Bill thinks that no one sees her leave.

Perhaps her sisters do what Bill tells them to do because they think she might pull the chain while they sit there. Sometimes Bill does steal up and pull the chain while one of them sits there quietly concentrating. Sometimes Bill puts insects down their backs. She chases the fat nanny around the lawn and tries to remove her *doek* because Bill wants to know what is underneath. The nanny pants and screams as she runs around the lawn, both hands to her head, hanging onto her white *doek*. The nanny always gives in in the end. Her sisters always give in in the end. Perhaps it is because of what they found in the earth under the oak tree.

She sits at the bottom of the garden in the shade of the oak tree, breathless. Everything is very still. She uses her pencil. She takes the blunt end of her pencil and pushes hard until she hears them fall back with a click. They always have china blue eyes.

Good! Good! Better like that.

Then she removes the rounded arms, the legs. She strokes the head with its painted hair, caresses it, dandles it. She sings a lullaby and kisses the pursed lips. She pulls off the ears. They always have those little rubber ears, which are cracked from going in the bath. She screws off the head with quick fingers. She scribbles on what remains, the swell of the stomach; she pokes the pencil into the place where there should be something else. She sticks her finger into the wound, tugs, frees herself. She digs a hole in the soft sand with a stick. She buries the torsos and the limbs and the head down in the garden under the oak tree by the dripping tap, where the narcissi grow in the spring, and the violets peep from the ground, where the earth is damp.

Bill tells Haze all the jacaranda trees in the garden are good except for the last tree on the left at the end of the alley. That one is bad, Bill says. "Why bad?" Haze asks.

"Because *Y* is a crooked letter and you cannot make it straight," Bill says.

She asks the Zulu servant why the banana tree that grows at the edge of the lawn bears no bananas. The Zulu servant says it is because the tree is a male and there is no female banana tree in the garden. He tells Bill that it is necessary to have both a male and a female banana tree to make bananas.

The house and the land, her mother inherited. Much of the food comes from the land. All the fruit—passion fruit, pomegranates, peaches, plums, nectarines, and lychees—all the vegetables—tomatoes, potatoes, parsnips, turnips, beans, gem squash—even the poultry and an occasional pig come from the land. With water, you can make anything grow in all this sunshine. The servants cost next to nothing.

All three girls sew. Even their mother sews. They tuck and smock and pleat. They do petit point. They make beaded handbags. They embroider tea cloths and tablecloths and doilies. They hem sheets. They crotchet all their blankets, their tea cozies, and the covers to the cushions in the lounge. They make lace for collars and cuffs. They make *lappies*, which hang on the line on certain days of the month. They knit bathing costumes with long legs that stretch when they go into the water and trail down their calves. They make all their own clothes. They make their underwear, their bloomers. They embroider their initials in pink or blue silk at the rim. They thread elastic through the legs with a safety pin. They make their own uniforms for school. They make dresses for their neighbors for pin money.

In the afternoons, after luncheon, Bill's mother lies down in the shuttered sickroom with the migraine. From the window on the staircase, Bill watches the doctor drive up to the house on straw that silences the wheels of the black victoria. He stops beneath the seringa tree. He hurries up the steps on short legs. He swings his fat black bag before him as he enters the hallway without knocking on the "stable" door. He unlatches the door himself.

From the top of the steps, Bill sees him pause in the hall, adjust his pearl tiepin before the mirror, smooth down his glossy hair, swell slightly, penguinlike in his shiny morning coat. He puffs out his plump chest. He stares at himself. He glances rapidly at the gray bowl of proteas and the shell-shaped china cups in the china cabinet before he hurries up the stairs. He stops only a moment on the stairs to grasp her chin and turn her face up to him. She does not smile. He stares down at her suspiciously with his bold, hard stare.

He stands by her mother's bed in the half dark of the sickroom, the cluttered room where they lie when they have the measles. It is a room with a rumpled bed and a standing mirror and a tapestry-covered armchair, a dressing table scattered with glass phials, photo frames, jars, a heart-shaped pincushion, and a small china Buddha on the glass top. In an alcove, potted plants cluster like mourners. Bill sees the outline of the doctor's body standing dark against the window. The doctor comes and holds her mother's hand and does as her mother asks him to do.

As she runs, Bill sees Haze's marmalade cat, Wurrypumpkin, who hunches in the shade of the barn while the cicadas shrill. His eyes are tightly closed, and he seems to sleep, but his tail beats the air from time to time like a whip.

This happens far from the house, where the earth is damp and dark because of the dripping tap and the deep shade of the oak tree. Narcissi grow here in the early spring. Light flickers through the leaves of the oak. Bill is crouching, playing with marbles in the damp earth, when Dottie jumps on her from behind. Dottie tumbles Bill onto the oozy earth and bites her on the nape of her neck. Dottie draws Bill's blood. She lies there, smelling the damp earth.

Sometimes in the night, faint and far, Bill thinks she hears the "stable" door close with a click. Once she thought she heard light footsteps outside the nursery door.

It is sultry indoors, but in the street sudden gusts of wind blow the dust about her. Her green tunic blows against her body as she runs to catch the tram. The light is white, the shadows dark, and the sky a glassy blue. The tram plunges along its burning metal arteries. The wheels touch off showers of yellow-red sparks. The tram clangs and shudders. When it stops, she throws herself forward to grasp at the handrail. She hoists herself aboard. Her body flutters as the tram lurches onward. She thinks that no one has seen her go.

According to Bill's mother, Bill was born at midnight, so the doctor told Bill's mother she could choose between the twelfth and the thirteenth as a birth date. She chose the thirteenth. She says Bill will bring her the luck she, Bill's mother, has never had in her life. She maintains she lies in her bed in the morning and dreams Bill has married a lord.

According to her mother, Bill was the only one of her three girls who would not let go of her breast. Bill sucked and sucked until her mother's breasts were cracked and sore.

Her mother says Bill needs a tonic to give her more color, despite the glow of her skin. Bill's mother says she has grown too fast, and that she looks a little anemic. Though Bill is never sick, never has so much as a sniffle or a slight headache or even the chicken pox, Bill's mother says the doctor should have a little look at Bill. Her mother says girls grow fast in this climate, that girls grow like sunflowers in the sun, that Bill has grown so fast because she is always outside running around in all this sun.

"When you lie, it is best to use as much truth as possible," Bill's mother says. She lies on her bed with what she calls the migraine and says, "Don't tell anyone everything, girls. Chest your cards." Bill's mother cheats at cards. Bill has watched her do it. When her relatives come to visit, Bill's mother makes the relatives sit facing the glare of the spring sun. The relatives are all called "Aunty" or "Uncle." They all look like crows with their dark glossy hair and their olive skins and their hard glittering eyes. They tilt their faces blindly in the sun until her mother offers them sunglasses. Bill's mother plays whist with her relatives for money. She stares into the relatives' sunglasses and sees their cards in the mirror of their glasses.

Bill sees Dottie standing at the open window in the early mornings, staring out at the dawn-lighted sky. Bill hears a bird make the call *Piet-my-vrou, Piet-my-vrou* and watches as Dottie bends her yellow arms, clenches her fists, and thrusts her elbows away from her flat chest. Dottie mutters as she does every morning, "I must, I must, I must increase my bust." Every night Dottie stands before the mirror, dabs calamine lotion on the spots she calls "mossie bites," and chants, "Out, out, damned spot." Bill, who has full breasts and never has any spots, listens to Dottie chanting and stares up at the stars.

·   ·   ·

As far back as Bill can remember, the light is there. It warms her shoulders; it muffles sounds; it casts dark shadows on the sand; it distances the world. She carries the light with her in her mind. Sometimes she shuts her eyes, tells her nanny to lead her, pretends to be blind. She walks with one hand stretched before her, head thrown back. Sometimes she plays blindman's buff with her sisters. Haze ties a cloth around Bill's eyes and turns her around and around. Giddy, Bill stumbles on the lawn, laughing, waving her hands wildly. At night, the moon shines. Even when it does not, she carries the jeweltree of stars in the darkness of her mind.

She watches her mother move in the pallid light of the moon. Her skin is whiter than wax. Bill tells her mother, "I have never seen anyone with such white skin except nuns."

Her mother puts her hand to her cheek, says, "It's the kind of skin that does not take the sun." She tells Bill she takes milk baths to keep her skin white, that Bill cannot be too careful in this climate, that she should wear cream, a hat in the sun.

In the green uniform and the panama hat with the green-and-black band around the rim, she sways back and forth. She is high up, elevated, riding the tram, beside the conductor. She has been told to keep her money in the pocket of her green bloomers, so she has to hitch up her skirt to pay for her ticket. The conductor smiles and glances at her leg and jokes with her. He says, "Next time you'll fall if you run so fast after the tram." He says she almost fell flat on her pretty face. She says, no, she will not, that it does not matter how fast she runs, she never falls. She pays for the ticket, which he punches. She laughs and jangles her bracelets and tosses the soft rope of her dark hair behind her. She looks out at a cloud moving across the sky. She looks at the dust blown up against the eucalyptus trees, at the walled houses and gardens with their fruit trees, their wisteria-covered *stoep*, their polished red steps, their pebbled glass doors. She thinks of the privies in the back. She sees the sun tap the helmet of a policeman, turn it to a turban, a burnoose.

When the tram stops, she notices a victoria, the top up, stopping behind the tram. She glimpses a gray glove, a face, and then there is nothing to be seen. For a moment, everything seems to come to a standstill. Everything is deadly quiet in the street. The street quivers in the heat. The sun blazes. A woman unfurls a black parasol.

Someone is watching her, she thinks; someone famous is following her. Perhaps it is the Queen on a visit to the colonies, the Queen leaning forward slightly in a hat with an ostrich feather, waving a gloved hand. Or it might be Cecil Rhodes, or the famous film star Bill goes to see in the afternoons, who has noticed her scent.

Slowly the victoria moves onward with the sad clipclop of the horse's hooves. Bill stares at the houses, pictures the shotgun passages that lead from the front doors to the back.

Once her father is called from the garden to get her loose. Her father strides down the shotgun passage into Bill's bedroom when she gets her head stuck between the brass bars at the end of the bed. Bill is dreaming on the bed in the afternoon, with the curtains drawn, dreaming of the horseman on the white horse, and her head gets stuck between the bars. Her father strides into the shuttered room. He stands facing her. She lies on her back, her head between the bars. She sees his face. Her father's face is the color of the red earth where the ants make their heap. His hair is russet. His mustache is stiff as straw. There are faded freckles on the backs of his thick hands. There are gold hairs. He places his hands on the bars of the bed and pulls, but he cannot spread them. Her head is stuck fast. Immovable. He sits down on the bed beside her. The springs of the narrow bed groan. He takes her by the shoulders and pulls at her. She can feel the bars digging into the sides of her head. She shouts, "Get me out of here! Get me out of here!"

He weeps. "How on earth did you get into this?"

At the bottom of the garden there is a dry, barren place where nothing but the hardiest shrubs grow. Only for a brief moment in the spring is the ground covered with wildflowers that spring from the bulb and then fade so fast, they leave behind nothing but a sweet fragrance that lingers a moment in the air.

Her mother seems hurried, as though she has been moving fast, is about to rush off somewhere, or has just rushed in from somewhere, as though she were rushed off her feet. She pants slightly after any sort of activity. Her small fingers tremble as she prongs her pearl-tipped hat pins into her flowered hats or pulls on her long kid gloves. Her white forehead is often damp. Her pale cheeks flush easily. Sometimes Bill thinks she hears, faint and far, her mother cry out in the night.

In the street, Bill wears her school uniform, with the sheer black stockings that show her shins scarred from picking at scabs. She runs to catch the tram, one hand to her hat despite the chewed elastic. In the street that day, look, she is no longer fat. She looks like all the other schoolgirls, like you, perhaps. A dry wind blows in gusts, and her skirt sucks at her body.

When her father gave her the money to buy school shoes, she went into town and bought a box of cream cakes. She ate them all coming down Bree Street in a victoria with the top down. At night she rose and went to the icebox and sucked the blood of the meat. She dipped thick slices of brown bread in the drippings from the roast.

After she saw the horseman on his Arab horse for the

first time, she stood naked before the standing mirror in the sickroom. She stared at her soft body in the mirror. Her eyes glowed dark and small in her fat face. She twitched her plump hips. She flapped her fat arms. She pouted her lips. She arched her back, thrust forward her breasts. Her hands haunted the hollows of her flesh, slipped between her thighs. She shut herself up in the sickroom and refused to eat. She starved until she was thin. No one recognized her in the street. She shed the fat as a snake sheds its skin in summer.

It lies sleeping in the shade. Under the agapanthi, near the driveway, Bill finds a snake curled up in the shade. She stares at the snake for so long and so hard, the light hurts her eyes, and she hardly sees the snake but sees herself, Bill-girl, lying in the shade. She hits the snake hard over the head with a stick. She watches it quiver, flick its body back and forth. Bill bangs the head methodically.

Good, better like that.

She watches her hands and the stick flicker in the sunlight. One moment, the body is writhing, and then she makes it lie still, just as she makes her mother appear in the early mornings and the sun rise at dawn beyond blue hills. Her hands lift the snake on the end of the stick up into the light. She watches the snake glisten in the light and hang down limply on either side of the stick. She smells the thin smell of rot and death.

She calls for the Zulu servant. She shouts, "John, come

quickly." She tells about the dead snake. The Zulu servant clucks his tongue and shakes his head and throws the snake onto the compost heap.

Bill climbs to the top of the ant heap and looks down at Haze. Bill puts her hands on her hips and shouts, "I am the king of the castle, and you are the dirty rascal."

She is not sure why they do as she tells them. She thinks it might be because her mother spoils her, or because her father favors her, or because Uncle Charles dotes on her. Sometimes she thinks it is because of her looks: the soft hazel eyes, the blue-black hair, the creamy complexion. But there are other girls with good looks. Surely it is not because they are afraid of her, constantly afraid of her even in the daylight?

It is hot and dark and airless in there. Big green flies buzz about Haze's head. It smells of Jeyes fluid in there. The stone floor is bare. Bill creeps up to the privy in *tackies* and pulls the chain and runs away fast while Haze is sitting there, concentrating, with her bloomers around her plump mosquito-bitten ankles. Haze jumps up. She runs out and leaves her bloomers on the stone floor. She screams, "The witch! The witch!"

If the witch catches you sitting there with your bloomers off while the chain is pulled and the water comes forth, who knows what she might do to you down there in the darkness?

. . .

Bill hides in the sickroom and places the standing mirror on the floor and sits on it. A girl at school told her what was supposed to be down there, and she wants to make sure it is. She sits on the mirror and stares at the wound.

On the tram, Bill sees thin plumes of smoke rising above the tin rooves from the chimneys of the houses on either side. Shade trees lean, and bougainvillea climb.

She lies on her bed between her sisters' beds and listens to the dawn wind jangling in the ragged leaves of the palm below her window. The black palm fronds toss in the wind, and the light pierces the leaves. The wind blows the wrack of white clouds from the sky.

Sometimes after luncheon, she lies on the bed and talks to the angel that stands at the end of the bed behind the brass bars. Bill lies naked in the dim light, only the white sheet over her. She skeins her hair into one thick dark plait. She sweats under the heavy hair that ropes down her back. Aloud she quotes, "I know a bank where the wild thyme grows."

Or she says, "Wake me early, Mother dear, for I'm to be Queen of the May."

Or she repeats the one Uncle Charles taught her: "Ooh la la, what is that mess that looks like strawberry jam? Hush, hush, my child, 'tis poor Papa run over by a tram!"

. . .

She hears the pebbled glass door bang. In the evenings, her father comes in through the back door and strides down the dim shotgun passage. He comes in from crossing his roses. He tells Bill he will come up with a new variety that he will name after her. He moves among the rose bushes in the twilight with thick, sad movements. Mostly the roses die. The crimson roses congeal into deep, fragrant clots.

In the servants' courtyard, there is noise. Chickens cluck, and dogs howl. In the evenings, there are guests, and her father complains that he has enough mouths to feed without having to feed the servants of the entire neighborhood, that he has enough difficulty borrowing from Peter to pay Paul without having to feed the entire neighborhood's servants.

In the evenings, Bill slips into the courtyard in her nightgown and stands barefooted against the brick wall of the house and watches. Men and women sip beer they have brewed; young women dance barefoot in the dust around the fire, their shoulders shaking. Bill watches the servants sip *skokiaan*. The alcohol makes them go mad, her mother says. Bill sees rage flicker in their eyes and in their rough gestures. She sees a man lift an ax toward a woman; the man's face is disfigured by the flickering light; the woman falls to her knees, her hands to her head. Bill sees the man's hands move back and forth and the ax catch the light from the fire;

blood streams from the deep gash across the woman's face.

The singing and the drunken shouts float through thin walls. Even with the window shut and the shade down, Bill can smell the smoke and the burning flesh.

They call her Bill because she behaves like a boy, because she climbs to the top of trees, plays football with the boys, gambles for marbles in the sand with the nanny's twins, and because she ties up her long, thick hair with a piece of string and pushes it under her straw hat. Before she saw the film where the horseman carries the woman across the sand, when she was still fat, they called her "fat white woman." They called out to her as she walked down the road: "Oh, fat white woman whom nobody loves, why do you walk through the fields in white gloves?"

It is not only the luncheons. They begin with breakfasts of chops or sausages, kippers or haddock cooked in milk, served with fried eggs and bacon or kidneys and buttered toast. They eat meat with every meal. They eat potatoes and rice and at least two green vegetables at midday and at night. They eat heavy steamed puddings accompanied by custard or stewed fruit. Not to mention the teas with cucumber sandwiches on beds of shredded lettuce and the cream cakes they eat in the late afternoons in the shadows on the lawn. Not to mention the chocolates Bill eats in the back bedroom with Uncle Charles in secret.

. . .

She throws her plait behind her. Her hair is so long, she can sit on it. Her hair is as black and as lustrous as an Oriental's. It is so black, it looks blue. The long rope of her plait swings back and forth. Her cheeks are rosy enough, but sometimes she slaps them to bring the blood into them and make her skin glow. The light is fierce and hard. Her shadow moves beside her on the grass. At first, she does not notice anyone else in the nearly deserted street.

Her mother asserts that Zulu boys make the best servants. She would never have a Zulu girl except as a nanny for the children. Zulu girls are too difficult to manage, her mother says.

Only Bill knows Zulu. She spoke it with the nanny before she learned English. Once she saw her mother wrinkle up her small nose and tell the ancient Zulu servant, who is almost blind, "Clean up this cupboard, John; it smells Zulu!" and the Zulu bowed his head, fell on his hands and knees on the floor of the cupboard, and cleaned.

" 'Onward, Christian soldiers, marching as to war,' " the Zulu servant sings as he stacks up all the furniture with the claws for feet in the middle of the room and blindly polishes the floors at dawn.

The afternoon sun flames the poinsettia, burnishes the oleander, and shines the lone blossom of a frangipani tree. The low walls are whitewashed. The gate is opened on the dust path that leads up to the house.

She keeps her eye fixed on her mother. If Bill does not hold her mother with her gaze, her mother will drift away, fly off, plunge and plummet, disappear. Her mother will be carried away by the witch.

Her mother lies in the sickroom and brushes out her long, lustrous hair. She twitches on her bed and rubs her little nose and her smoky blue-green eyes. The air in the sickroom is heavy and bittersweet. The room smells of lavender and verbena and the bitter herb her mother soaks for her constipation. Her mother moans of her clotted insides, her immovable bowels. She orders, "Dottie, hurry up and call the doctor." Or her mother wails, "This place is going to rack and ruin. Everything is tumbling down. The locusts are eating the plants again."

Bill watches from the shadows of the sickroom. She sits cross-legged on the floor behind the potted plants and watches until her mother remembers her and tells her to go and see whether Uncle Charles is in his room and not wandering around the garden, as he was the time her father found him under the hydrangeas with a knife, hunting for Boers. Bill leaves the room but lingers in the corridor and watches in the standing mirror by the door.

She can hear her mother asking the doctor to help her sleep. Bill can hear her mother pleading softly.

The doctor clears his throat and mutters, "Now, now, we all have our cross to bear." He massages her mother's forehead with the square tips of his fat fingers. Bill can see the doctor's fingers jumping about like toads in the mud of her mother's dark hair. Bill can see the toads hopping toward the white mound of the breast.

Once a week or sometimes more than once, when her father has left the house, the doctor pays her mother a call in his shiny suit, his shiny black shoes, his gold fob watch, and his increasing embonpoint. He bends his handsome head, and his cheeks glow. He takes out his plump fountain pen from the silk pocket on the inside of his morning coat. He writes on his thick pad and signs his name with a flourish. Bill knows what he writes. He always writes the same thing.

She watches him hurry down the steps and out of the house. She listens to the horse's hooves going clippedy-clop down the street.

At dusk, her father plays Chopin waltzes in the lounge. She waits for him to come in through the back door from the half-lit garden. He takes off his yellow gardening gloves slowly as he walks down the shotgun passage from the back garden and into the lounge. Bill sits on the tapestried piano bench and cushions her head on his shoulder while he plays on the upright piano. He throws back his head. The light falls on the freckles on his hands. His hands lift and hover there and alight on the keys.

Her family expects one thing of her, but she is already another. They try to trap with silken nets. What Bill likes to do in the afternoons is to slip away and ride the tram along R. Street. She likes to sit in the half dark and watch the horseman and wander the streets alone at dusk.

Bill's father says the men who flocked to this place were not looking for open spaces. What they were looking for was the gold in the earth. The Uitlanders came with pick, shovel, and pan. Overnight they built a city of narrow streets and buildings, huddled close. During the day, it was a noisy place, filled with the sudden cries of Indian vendors, of drunken men, and the chanting of the bare-footed newspaper boys. At night it became a city of pleasure. Dust and lime and scaffolding were every-where. Something was always being put up or taken down. Dust from the mine dumps webbed the leaves of the eucalyptus trees and coated the wheels of the vehicles. In the summer heat, the streets smelled unpleasant. Gold light streamed in swaths between the dusty trees. The palm fronds beat with a dry sound, and dust rose in the air.

Someone is following her down the street in a victoria, she thinks. Some mysterious personage is following the tram. Perhaps it is Uncle Charles's hero, Cecil Rhodes, she thinks, though, of course, Cecil Rhodes is dead. Perhaps someone has seen her and wants to put her on the stage or in a film. Not that she is unaccustomed to this. The one who is following her is not the first to follow her in the street. There have been others.

Bill watches from the window on the stairs. She watches the black victoria approaching the house. She sees the doctor descend, look up at the window where she sits on the stairs. The doctor stops on the stairs and gazes down at Bill suspiciously. He has found her reading what he writes for her mother on his little pad. Bill has read the mark from the pen. The doctor does not know what to make of Bill, but she knows what to make of him.

The sisters whisper about it. Dorothy and Hazel and Bill shut themselves in the nursery and sit close on the brass bed. They put their heads together and whisper about their mother. Dorothy and Hazel say their mother is sometimes "silly." This is the word they use for the times when she withdraws, when their mother becomes someone else; she no longer hears them, notices them; she hardly knows who they are; she confuses their names, calls Bill Dottie, or she runs their names all together; DozeBill, she calls them. Her eyes glaze over; her lips close firmly like a lily on a fly; she turns as white as paper; she floats somewhere else; she disappears. It is from something they do not know the name of. Bill knows the name.

It was Bill's grandfather who bought the land for almost nothing. Her mother says that he all but stole it from a miner down on his luck. Until Bill was an adolescent there was no sewer system, just a privy in a shed behind the house. When the wind blew toward the house, the stench reached it and filled the rooms.

In the yellow-green shadow of the oak trees, she is raking the earth around the compost heap. It is cool under the oak trees. She can smell the rotting compost. She can hear the green flies buzzing and see their shiny wings. The rake is rusty. She plunges it into her foot. The rake bends back the flesh between her toes. For a moment, she is not able to move. The light keeps shifting through the leaves of the trees. Then she twists the rake deeper into her flesh. She watches the blood spurt, and then seep slowly into the earth.

The Principessa C whispers something into Bill's ear. The French teacher, who claims she married an Italian prince, draws Bill aside after class.

In the afternoons, the Principessa C, who has a trunk like a barrel on little short legs, tells the girls, "Pull down the blinds. I want to tell you something." She lowers her voice and says she was tortured in the war; she had her nails pulled out; she was plunged into boiling and freezing water by the Huns. She says the Huns are barbarians who rip the heads off babies. She says the Huns rip off unmentionable parts of men's bodies and eat them.

The French teacher, who is actually Belgian, draws Bill aside and asks Bill to tell her when it is her time of the month.

She wears the summer uniform, though it is not yet summer. She wears the panama hat with the brim turned up all around so that her flower face is visible. She tilts the hat back on her head. She does not fear the heat of the sun. The dark curls that escape from her plait cling to her damp forehead and neck. She is still panting from the running. Her cheeks are flushed. She laughs a little when the conductor speaks to her. She slips her triple copper bracelets up her rounded arm. As she brings her arm down, the bracelets fall about her wrist. Her bracelets jangle as she lowers her arm to look for her money. Her thin blouse, she knows, shows the outline of her breasts as she leans forward to take out her money. The pleated skirt of her tunic sways against her plump thighs with the movement of the tram. She wears the regulation lace-up shoes and the black stockings, but the stockings have laddered; they show her pink flesh. Her ankles and the strong curve of her calves are visible. She stands feet apart. She sways back and forth with the movement of the tram. The conductor looks at her leg.

Bill's mother says that the right clothes can change your life. She says your clothes should be elegant and fashionable if you are to get anywhere. She says that tangles in your hair and runs in your stockings will never get you anywhere. She believes that fine feathers make fine birds.

Bill makes her way from her bed while everyone sleeps. She finds her way into the sickroom by the light of the moon. She fetches the scissors from the dressing table drawer. She stands in the half dark of the nursery, the scissors hanging in her hand, and listens to the even breathing of her sisters. She looks at Dottie's open, avid mouth. Bill stares at the dress on the back of the cupboard door in the moonlight. The window is open, and the long red net skirt billows darkly. The cherries rustle softly. Bill cuts off each bunch of crepe cherries. She can hear the crunch of the steel scissors and the soft fall of the crepe cherries at her feet. She watches the red cherries fall, one by one, to the floor. She cuts off each bunch of crepe cherries her mother sat up all night to sew on the dress Dottie was to wear when she sang "Cherry Ripe" at the eisteddfod.

Uncle Charles's room is small and dark. It looks over the back garden, shaded by the fig tree that grows close to the house. There are fat brown leather chairs, worn on the arms, and a leather sofa with a striped blanket spread across cushions. When you sit on the cushions, you can hear the air escaping. Bill likes the sound of the singing birds he keeps in painted cages that hang from the windows and from the ceiling. There are canaries and budgerigars that hop and flutter their wings. There is a budgerigar called Coca that sits on Uncle Charles's shoulder and chirps, "Coca-Cola, Coca-Cola," and pecks at his cheek. Sometimes the bird hops onto his head, perches in the cloud of his thick white hair, and pecks.

She sees someone she thinks she knows who follows the dust and the screeching tram and her long, swinging braid.

She likes the sound of the tram. She likes the creak, the clang, the yaw. She likes the swaying and rocking as it hurtles down steep streets. She likes to watch the sparks fly from beneath the wheels and to taste the dust and burning metal in her mouth. She likes the stares of the people in the tram.

" 'Lift thine eyes, oh lift thine eyes, to the hills.
 " 'Whence cometh, whence cometh, whence cometh my help.' " They sing at school. They pray on their knees, eyes shut, sweating in the heat, for the girls in the sister school of the same name in England. The girls all sing, " 'And did those feet in ancient time walk upon England's

mountains green?' " and their hair bristles on the backs
of their legs.

When the grass turns brown and the nights cold, the
spinster teachers all clasp their hands and sigh, saying,
" 'Oh, to be in England, now that April's there.' " Bill's
mother speaks of England as "home," though neither
Bill's mother nor Bill's mother's mother has ever been
there.

When Bill asks when they will use the cups locked in
the china closet, her mother draws herself up and says,
"When the Queen comes to tea." Bill sees the Queen
with an ostrich feather in her hat, sitting in the dark
lounge, her hand on the dim embroidered doilies on the
arm of the chair, sipping tea from a transparent cup,
inclining her head graciously toward Bill.

Sometimes Dottie and Bill and Haze play a game called
Darling. They call one another "darling" and drink tea
out of cups, their little fingers lifted high in the air. They
wipe the corners of their mouths with handkerchiefs,
simpering, "But, darling, how *could* you, after all I have
done for you?" Or, "*Darling*, if you only knew how much
I *worry* about you."

Bill strikes up a pose from the cinema. Her mother
watches her and says, "Who do you think you're being
now, Clara Bow?"

Bill puts her hands over her ears. "Which role are you

playing now?" her mother asks her. Bill puts her hands over her eyes.

She listens to the uproar in the street, watches the motor-cars shoot by the tram, watches the black victoria follow-ing, led by a black horse.

She watches a crowd of satcheled schoolgirls wind their way down the street, double-file. They look as she does. She could be one of them, except for the brown of their uniform, the scent.

The girls at school can make themselves do it. Bill works at it, but she is never able to bring it off, though she pretends. At early communion, before breakfast, the girls hold their breaths and then breathe out hard. They slump back from the altar in a swoon, with the host on their tongues. When the priest says, "The body of Christ . . . eat," they turn back their eyes and escape themselves. They swoon and have to be carried out into fresh air.

It is Miss Killy who has to carry them out of chapel into the garden. She rises to her big feet. She bears down the aisle valiantly to sweep up the swooning girl. Miss Killy is a strapping young woman who comes from Wales. Once she went walking in the mountains there and came back to school tanned with the reflected light of the snow. "She's as brown as a native," all the girls whispered, giggling.

Bill can only pretend to swoon at communion. She leans on Miss Killy's arm heavily as they walk down the flagged aisle of the chapel with the shafts of light shining vivid blue and yellow through stained-glass.

Uncle Charles slumps on the leather couch, his long legs crossed in threadbare khaki trousers. A leather slipper dangles from his toe. He has a strange vacant air. He has deep-set eyes in a bony face and bushy eyebrows and clammy hands. He gives his Bill-girl chocolates to eat from a black box with the picture of a white bow across the top. There are three layers of chocolates. She looks at the diagram on the inside of the cover and first eats the square ones with the toffee in the center from each of the layers, then she works on the rest. While she eats, Uncle Charles talks about the Boer War in his deep voice.

He says the diamond town could easily have been taken during the siege, but the Boers believed there were mines around the limits of the town. They were afraid to cross the mines, which did not exist, he maintains. According to Uncle Charles, the Boers are idiots, uncouth barbarians. He says they are brutes who hunt in packs, that they beat the natives with *shamboks* and have hair on their backs, and that they all sleep in one bed. Father, mother, and child all sleep in one big bed, he tells Bill. While he talks, his gaze is fixed on the floor in a gloomy stare, and his hand strays. His quick fingers flutter like a bird.

. . .

Bill's mother says it is difficult to explain, because Bill knows so little about life, so little about men. Bill says she knows enough about men, that she knows all she wants to know about men.

She imagines someone watches her descend and go into the cinema. But once inside, she forgets about everything. In the cool half dark of the cinema, she watches the horseman sweep across white sand. She sits in the flickering light and the smoke and watches the horseman ride across the sand.

She can hear the sound of the piano as she steps up to the window to buy her ticket at The Bijou. The film has begun as she walks into the flickering light of the hall and finds a seat near the front. She sits in there, her knees apart, a packet of sweets—pink-and-white hearts and diamonds—in the hollow of her lap. She leans forward, her arms crossed on the seat in front of her, stares at the screen, breathes softly. She watches the horseman gallop across the sand. The wind blows the sand that has been kicked up and blows the man's flowing robes.

The flickering light makes the hall seem unreal. There is only the flickering light, the horseman galloping across the sand, and the sound of the piano. She hears the woman with the gray wig run her hands up and down the piano keys. The woman sways back and forth. She goes suddenly from a diminuendo to a crescendo. Bill knows the story by heart. She has seen the film many times. Many times she has watched the horseman sweep across the desert. She thinks she will never see anything as lovely in her whole life. She watches the man lift the struggling woman into his arms, carry her off across the sand on his white horse in white light.

In the shade of the mulberry trees, in the soft sand at the bottom of the garden near the bamboo shoots and the fish pond, Bill feeds the nanny's twins chocolates she has slipped into the pocket of her bloomers in Uncle Charles's room. Sometimes she makes them do things with one another. She and the nanny's twins are the same age. They learned English together. The first language Bill learned was Zulu. Then she learned Xhosa. She learned to click her tongue on the roof of her mouth. She makes the twins call her *Inkoos* or *Nkulu* chief.

Uncle Charles calls from his window, "Want a chocolate, Bill-girl?" Once one of Uncle Charles's birds lay in the corner of its cage, a bead of blood on its open beak. Uncle Charles's favorite bird lay dead, its head twisted against the bars of its cage.

In the afternoons, Bill escapes from the house with its cramped rooms, its odor of stale female flesh and eau de cologne, and the unrelenting heat of its corrugated iron roof. She catches the tram to go and watch the horseman ride wildly across the sand in the glare of white light. Afterward she lingers in the streets. Men follow her.

Her mother tells Bill she has such a longing for the past, for her life as a girl. She says Uncle Charles was rather a dull boy, you know, a little simple, always a little slow, perhaps, but sometimes, it seems to her now, he was the only man in her life. Bill's mother calls the color of Uncle Charles's eyes cornflower blue.

Sometimes in the night, Bill thinks she hears a cry coming from the end of the long corridor, from the sickroom, where her mother now sleeps alone.

Now, look, see her lean back in the wooden chair and smoke a cigarette. She takes the smoke into her lungs in deep inhalations. She watches the smoke coil in the light of the projector. She does not pay attention to the elderly ladies in the front row who nod and mutter, half-asleep under flowered hats. She does not care that the elderly ladies turn to stare at her from time to time, or that they wonder what a girl in school uniform is doing in the cinema at that hour in the afternoon, sucking sweets and smoking and watching the man ride across desert sand.

She watches the horseman's pointed ears. She sees his nose is perfectly straight in profile but notices a curve when he faces the camera. The famous face flickers, lips parted, eyes flashing; the form seems to dissolve in the desert glare.

Only later, when she comes out of the cinema, does she realize that someone is still looking for her in the lengthening shadows of the street. Someone, not a stranger, is looking for her in the red light of the setting sun and the swift coming of the starlit night.

She likes his burning eyes, the way he draws back his lips. She likes the way he puts his hand on his hip, the whorls of his turban, the curve of the dagger thrust into the belt. She likes the way the woman he holds in his arms throws back her head and struggles in vain. Bill likes the shimmer of light in the woman's hair, on the clear oval of her face. Bill likes the woman's abject gaze.

The girl in the green uniform comes out of the cinema and stands in the shade of the marquee. She listens to the myriad sounds of the square—cars, wagons, footsteps on the pavement behind her.

She strolls slowly past the gray railing. She saunters down Bree and Rissik streets. She walks just to walk. She navigates through the crowds of people like a boatsman. She lets the current catch her up and sweep her onward, then turns and thrusts against the tide. She steers through waves of light and shadow. Her body whirls.

People pass, looking at her. It is a look she has begun to recognize. It is all a show, just for her: the newspaper boys, the beggars, drunken men falling out of bars, the trees, the high-pitched piping of a penny whistle, even the pale half-moon visible in the light sky.

She watches the glass windows fragmenting the light, the electric tram, the omnibuses, the rickshas, the victorias, the motorcars, the open lorries filled with dusty black men in rags who cling on around the curves, the mingling crowds, the shop windows with their thin, white mannequins, their gleaming silver, their jewels, the fish-and-chips shops, the betting parlors, the bars. She has conjured it up, brought it forth, drawn up the iron latticework of the gold town, the plate-glass windows, the post-office clock, just as she makes her mother step forth into the dawn.

Through thin walls, Bill hears the doctor say something about constant surveillance. Her father says, "At that price, it better be constant."

The doctor goes on, "Most devoted and diligent."

Bill's father remarks, "I am all for diligence." Her father says something Bill cannot hear. "No alternative," the doctor states. She hears something fall to the floor and roll. The doctor says, "An admirable person, I assure you, quite admirable." Bill hears the doctor assure her father that he, the doctor, always chooses his nurses himself in cases like these. He says he visits as often as possible to keep an eye on things.

She hurries onward with her head lowered in the dull light. She is not afraid of strangers, but she watches out for thieves. She goes down the narrow street. She hears the quick tap-tap of the footsteps coming closer, sounding louder and louder in the quiet of the street. The street seems very long. Her shoes rub her heels; she stumbles on the fissured pavement. Finally she turns.

She remembers following her mother down a narrow street in the gold town. Bill remembers her mother's glossy hair in ringlets under the hat with the ostrich feather, the corseted figure, the slim ankles in the high boots, the frilly parasol. Her mother strides on with her head back, her legs reaching out across the gray pavement. Bill can see herself following with difficulty, hurrying on short, fat legs, hanging back, dragging on her mother's arm in a tucked dress, with straight dark hair and a fringe on her forehead, trying to keep up and at the same time to avoid the lines on the pavement where the witch lurks.

Summer

All her life, she will remember her mother sleeping, always sleeping, with the curtains closed on the light in the hot summer afternoons, her arm flung across her face, as though sleep were a lover she was embracing.

Look at Bill. She is doing it again. She is slipping down the stairs, with the sun at its height, passing through the dark hall, stepping out into summer light. She is going through the garden again, running in the summer heat.

Waves of heat rise from white stones. Heavy leaves hang down, shining and still as metal. Sun and sky are scattered on the grass. A blue pigeon circles in the sky above her as she runs down the street in the vapid haze, along the whitewashed wall, past the fruit trees. She lingers in the shadow of a plum tree, takes a stick of rouge from her pocket, paints her lips, rubs them together, spreads the rouge on her cheeks with quick fingers. She goes on running across the fissured pavement, head held high like a fist.

At the Christmas luncheon, she watches, kicks at the table leg, waits. The family lingers. They pick at the hot dishes brought through the swing door by the blind servant, who bangs the dishes against the mahogany sideboard: the great Christmas turkey roasted to a crisp gold-brown, decorated with a sprig of fictive holly, the sweating Christmas pudding, stuffed with handfuls of silver coins. Bill's father pants as he carves the turkey. He sweats as he flames the Christmas pudding, the flame invisible in the gold light, the cotton-wool snow on the Christmas tree gold, the only kind of snow Bill has ever seen. She is looking through the pudding on her plate, searching with a spoon, hunting for silver. When she chews the Christmas pudding gingerly, she bites on a silver coin, which is bitter on the tongue.

The family is finally leaving the table. The mother is retiring to the sickroom to sleep. Dottie and Haze are wandering out under the willow tree to play the gramophone. Bill is running alone along the street, the shadow at her back.

She is wearing the low-waisted summer frock of something so soft, so thin, she feels it ripple as she runs. She plunges through light like a diver through water. She seems to be running in water. In the stuff she is almost naked, she knows. The low sash shows off her hips, her thighs, her knees. She slows down to adjust the sash, to glance behind her, to lift an arm to wave to her sisters, who are playing the gramophone. She catches a glimpse of Haze dozing, pink and brown, her round head in Dottie's lap. Bill sees the sun fling spangles through the leaves on Haze's plump legs in the grass. Dottie waves back to Bill as she runs by the whitewashed wall. Dottie sings along with the singer in her thin voice.

" 'I'm the Sheik of Araby.

" 'Your love belongs to me.

" 'At night when you are fast asleep, into your tent I creep.' "

In the summer heat, the garden is very still. Something has strangled the wind. The roses hang their heavy heads. The sun streaks them with bands of light. The pale mauve blossoms have fallen, leaving the pinnate leaves trembling on the jacaranda trees. Bill sees a woman in a white uniform in the distance, walking arm in arm with a man in a morning coat. The woman seems to float in the heavy air. The man bends his head toward her in the haze.

In the Christmas months at the height of the heat, there is no school. It is the long Christmas holiday. Bill rises late, lingers in the nursery, the hot, low-ceilinged room. It is painted a pale green, with a blackboard along one wall, brass beds, mosquito nets, chamber pots in the bottom of bedside tables, and a bay window that opens onto the garden below. When the sun streams in aslant through the blinds in the early morning, she likes to climb up into the well of the open window. She breathes in the smell of the earth coming up from the garden below.

Sitting there in her white nightgown, barefooted, eating thick cold sausages saved from breakfast for her by her sisters, she hears the gramophone. Dottie and Haze are lolling on the lawn under the willow tree, playing the gramophone. The sound reaches Bill weakened and indistinct. She leans her forehead against the sash of the window and looks out across the lawn at the street where the tram stops.

She sees only the horseman cast by her imagination, riding into light and dust. She rubs her face in her loose hair, breathes in the warm dusty scent; lifts her arm to her face, smells the skin at the back of her wrist, sticky with sleep. She licks at it, laps at her creamy skin. She bends down, touches her face to her bare knee, kisses the inside of her knee, smells the faint odor of sleep. She is dreaming of the horseman and smelling herself.

. . .

In the daylight darkness, Bill watches the woman in the white uniform, who sits beside her mother's bed with her back to the wall, her face glistening damply. In the blue light of the sickroom, the woman looks like a ghostly shadow.

The woman follows Bill down the corridor and finds her in her father's bathroom with his razor in her hand. The woman says, "What have you got there? What have you got in your hand? Are you listening to me?" The woman adds, "What on earth are you doing with your father's razor?"

Bill folds the blade back into the handle, slips the razor into the pocket of her bloomers, and looks the woman in the white uniform in the eye. Bill's gaze makes the woman blink her pale yellow eyes.

In the evenings, when dusk falls sudden as a knife, Bill watches her mother as she wanders out through the French doors into the garden, holding her arms out before her. Her mother paces the path above the rock garden, silvered. The moon is on her like water. She is walking white, silver-shined by moon. Clouds pass across the face of the moon for a moment, obscuring her; then they move free. Bill makes her mother reappear, makes her glide across the lawn. Bill glazes the garden, makes the flowers shine white, the trees glow silver. She stands beside her mother in the shadows among the jacaranda pods and watches the house and the garden rise and fall.

. . .

In the house on R. Street at the height of the summer, the door to the sickroom is left ajar. Bill finds her mother sleeping there, sleeping deeply, as if in a swoon, one arm flung across her face, a sheet half-covering her wasted body. Caught in the sharp wedge of light that pierces a chink in the curtain, the arm looks separate, flung there by accident, a stranger's.

Her mother sleeps her drugged sleep in the dead world of the sickroom all through the hot days; she goes on sleeping until the fall of dusk awakens her. In the evenings, she rises, mothlike, when the lamps are lit.

When the first light of evening falls upon the garden, the family drifts onto the white veranda. Bill's mother saunters outside in her low-waisted crepe dress and pointed shoes. The breeze flutters at her hem. She stretches out in a straw chair languidly and sips gin and tonic under the yellow lights and stares at the plants dying for want of water and from the constant heat.

Bill watches her mother dab her forehead and her eyes with a handkerchief. She murmurs, "I cannot help wondering what Maud was thinking at the end, at that last moment, before her body—"

"Now, now," Bill's father interrupts, rising.

Bill's mother says, "But there must have been an instant, don't you think, when she saw the tree looming up and knew?"

Uncle Charles sits in the shadows and smokes a cigarette and says to Bill's mother, "You have always re-minded me of Maud, you know."

Bill's mother says, "I cannot help seeing her thin ankles and her thin wrists against the dashboard."

Bill's father faces about and back again, his hands be-hind his back. "Pull yourself together, for God's sake."

Bill's mother says, "Snapped," and rubs her thin fingers around her thin wrist.

Sometimes in the summer afternoons, Bill dresses up as a bride. She weaves garlands of the yesterday-today-and-tomorrow flowers, with their waxy smell of dead time and their giddy promise of tomorrow. She wears them about her neck, her ankles, her wrists. She places red hibiscus behind her sisters' ears to show they are the grooms. Together they walk across the lawn, past the poinsettia bushes, past the jasmine. She leads them along the dust path beside the white wall, where the salmon and crimson bougainvillea leap like brilliant flames.

Sometimes she has them push her in the wheelbarrow, though it is the soles of *her* feet that are hard; it is she who can walk across the pebbles of the driveway without flinching. She has them push her across the blazing lawn down to the abandoned victoria in the shed and makes them play Doll in the dim light. Her sisters are the dolls.

She makes them climb into the back of the victoria and lie on the leather seat in the shadows and take off their clothes. One of them is on her back and the other on top and both of them making little moans. "Now, now, we all have our cross to bear," says one, and the other, "If you only knew how much I *suffer*." She watches the toads hop.

You can hear the clang of the tram, the rattle. You can see the tram approaching in the distance. Bill is running again, sunlight in her eyes. See how easily she runs through the white gate, through the white light, the dream light.

"Go on, do it," they beg her in the white light of the lamp. With the curtains open on the jeweltree of stars in the southern sky, Bill stands very straight before the mirror, tilts her head to one side, sees her sisters behind her, and arches an eyebrow inquiringly.

"I'll give you my garnet cross," Dottie promises. Her sisters sit on the bed and watch as Bill unbuttons her white nightdress slowly. She drops her arms, and with a shake of her shoulders, lets her nightdress fall open on her white breasts. She watches her sisters watching her. Haze gasps. Bill folds down the top of her nightdress, ties it around her waist, gazes at them solemnly. She rises on her toes, twirls, leaps. They let out a soft sound that echoes out toward the stars and the far reaches of the veld.

They sew to keep up appearances. They alter dresses for pin money. They sit up at night in the hot rooms under the tin roof and take down hems in the light of the lamp. They remove sleeves, let out waists, attach mother-of-pearl sequins in the shape of stars and moons onto the bodices of evening dresses; they put up hems.

They are putting up the hem of the woman's red dress. The stout woman is turning on the dining room table. The dark mahogany glistens in the light of the lamp. The fleshy feet are strangled in tight shoes that shuffle on the table. The blue-marbled legs move so slowly, they seem almost still, thick pillars. Everything seems still. Bill removes a pin from the hem of the skirt with quick fingers and pushes hard until she hears a little shriek.

Good! Good! Better like that.

She goes on pushing the pin into the thick pillar, into the blue-marbled sinew. The shrieking goes on. She watches the woman rolling her eyes ridiculously, as if she were exaggerating pain, mimicking it. The woman hops and hobbles around the table. Like a puppet, she jerks comically, her big mouth open in surprise. She stands there shaking dramatically, a fake.

While they work, Bill's mother sits in the shade of the laburnum tree and sews with shaky hands and mutters about not throwing their lives away, the way she has hers.

Over the grandfather clock in the lounge, the angels lift their trumpets aloft. On the wall in the nursery, the cuckoo breaks through its wooden doors. The thin bronze clock in the dining room ticks loudly in the stillness of the house. The travel clock glows green beside her mother's bed. The pendulum of the brass clock in the hall swings from side to side.

Bill likes to watch the black hands of the clocks turning so slowly she can hardly discern the movement. The hands move like exhausted explorers across desert sand, stumbling along one behind the other, dragged along one by the other, inching from oasis to dark oasis. The beating of her heart mingles with the ticking of the clocks.

She hears someone calling out as if from afar. The water slapping against the sides of the pool, the cicadas, the chattering in the changing rooms muffle the sound of the voice calling out. Perhaps some of the girls who are chattering also hear someone calling out but think it is a game. The girl, the swimming captain, the one who is in the class above Bill, the one who showed Bill how to do it, is sinking, rising, and calling out. Bill hears the sound, but the sun beats down hard on her shoulders and holds her back like a hand.

Bill stands on white tile in the bathroom and asks, "Will I grow older than Dottie?"

Her mother smiles and replies apologetically, "You might grow taller, Pet."

"Why can I never grow older, if I want to?" Bill says, and studies the shadow on the floor.

"Because *Y* is a crooked letter and you cannot make it

straight," her mother replies, and lifts her hands to her head. "Such a pain here," she says. "Such a pain."

She finds her way by memory through the shuttered house as if in some underground place. She stands in the long hallway outside the sickroom and listens. She hears her mother and the doctor murmuring. The doctor's voice is louder. Bill hears him admonish, "Come, come, be reasonable, my dear." Her mother pleads. The doctor clears his throat. "Of course, I will always be here for you, Temple."

Her mother calls out, "Pet, are you there? I know you are out there, Pet. You might as well come in here. Come in here a moment, won't you, Pet?" Bill kicks at the baseboard with her lace-up shoe. Then she enters the half dark of the room, stands very still in the shadows, palms behind her, pressed to the wall, smelling the soaking herbs.

The room is very warm because the curtains and the windows are closed. The plants wilt. There is hardly any light in here. Here and there, motes move in a beam. Night seems interminable.

Bill's mother lies on the bed, her face gray. Her face twitches. She rubs her eyes and fidgets with her loose hair. The doctor bends over her proprietorially. His glossy hair gleams. Bill studies his physiognomy to see if there is any trace of blue shadow on his chin, but his chin looks smooth and pale. He glances at the woman in the white uniform, who is arranging the glass bottles on the round table among the potted palms. The bottles clink.

Her mother tells Bill how she, Bill's mother, lost her mother in the dark, when they hid in the mine shafts during the siege of the diamond town. Her mother says she saw a native girl carrying a bundle of washing on her head walk down the street and have her head blown clean from her shoulders. "A bullet blew her head and the washing onto the ground," her mother says. She tells Bill the thing she can never forget is the way the force of the bullet made the bundle of washing and the head shoot up in the air and then fall at some distance from where the native girl lay.

Bill hears the approaching tram, sees the poinsettia bushes—slashes of blood red—as she runs to catch the tram. She sees the charred veld laid waste by summer fires. She can taste the acrid smoke on her tongue. She senses that someone is following her again.

Men follow Bill in the street. They follow her scent. They follow her, she thinks, not because of her dark eyes or creamy complexion or long dark hair but because of her scent. She carries a little bottle of scent in her pocket, dabs scent behind her ears, her wrists, on the tip of her tongue. Her skin shimmers damply in the heat. The heat brings out the scent. She knows; she can smell it. They can even smell her in the rain. They follow her when the summer storms break at dusk and cool the air. They follow her as far as the house on R. Street. They stand in the dark, dripping garden, smelling her and staring up through the hot mist at the windows. She feels their eyes out there in the wet darkness, watching. They watch her move from room to lighted room. They watch her jumping naked on the bed and singing: " 'Sometimes in the summer time, sometimes in the fall, I jump between the linen sheets, with nothing on at all.' "

There is an aviator who flies over the house on R. Street and drops love notes into the garden. They flutter down into the flowers. She finds the love notes among the nasturtiums, the foxgloves, the sweet williams. She parcels her suitors out between her sisters. She says, "Haze, you can have this one."

It is a bright afternoon, a wanton day, rife with the threat of increasing heat. Clouds melt in the heat; shadows spill beneath them across the asphalt. The sun blazes and blazes. The streets are a furnace. It is hot, hot, the heat of hell. Bill stops in the street, looks up into the sky, imagines the stars there, cool behind the blue vault.

She walks on carelessly as though she ignores the dangers of the street, ignores the shadow at her back.

Bill watches the woman in the white uniform stand in the long, hot corridor, her full figure lit by the blue light from the half-opened door of the sickroom. She leans against the wall, her uniform too tight for her in the right places. She lifts her head toward the doctor when he lights her cigarette with a quick-firing flame. Her eyes look almost shantung yellow; they gleam fiercely. She is handsome, Bill thinks, and young, or quite young, though Bill has no way of knowing her age. Bill watches her draw the smoke deep into her lungs and let it out slowly between uneven teeth, removing a fleck of tobacco from the tip of her tongue. The woman blinks and says in a deep, husky voice, "These children would be better off in an orphanage." The doctor lifts his hand toward his small mouth, glances in Bill's direction, and whispers, "Little pitchers have big ears."

Her sisters follow her down the dust path on summer days. They traverse the hot lawn, the humped wooden stile. Haze says, "It's too hot, Bill. I want to go home," and hangs back.

Bill says, "Oh, come on, Haze."

Bill leads her sisters across burning veld, through empty spaces where tins and rubbish glint in the stiff grass. They cross the flat field, blackjacks catching in their short socks, making their way into the shade of a mulberry tree, where Bill sees a white butterfly turn blue in the shadow.

They are looking up into the dark leaves with serrated edges that they feed to the silkworms in science class at school. They are gazing at the bloodred fruit. They pick the mulberries and crush them with their fingers and palms. They tip back their heads and squeeze the berries so that the juice trickles down their fingers into their mouths, some of it running over their chins. They take off their shoes and tuck up their skirts and push up their sleeves in the noonday sun. They smear mulberries on one another's faces and limbs. Haze's pigtail turns a wild scarlet. Dottie weeps red tears. They hold hands and do a war dance—is it the Zulu war dance? They bend their knees and pound the hot earth with their bare feet.

As far back as Bill can remember, the wild storms are there in the summer nights. She climbs into the window seat and pushes open the window so that she can hear the sounds of the storm. Hail rattles hard like bullets on the corrugated iron roof. Thunder rumbles close upon her. Lightning cracks overhead. Bill gazes unblinkingly at the night sky. The lightning forks, brighter than sunlight, illuminating the sky. The house is lit up for a moment, all the white rooms, the sickroom, the long hallway, the nursery, made suddenly luminous.

When the lightning illuminates the sky, Bill sees the pale oval of Haze's face beside her. Haze holds on to Bill. They stare out into the hot dripping garden and breathe in the bitter odor of wet earth.

In the morning mist, the dark blue hills look like islands, and bone white birds lift and fall in the distance. They fall asleep with the dawn. Dottie wakes them, entwined. She says, "You two are acting like lovers."

. . .

Riding the tram is like riding a horse. Bill sways from side to side to the movement of the tram. She rocks, she leans, she lists. The heat makes her feel flushed, makes her gaze ahead wearily. Her mother says it is the heat that makes girls grow up fast out here, that makes them so wild, so reckless.

Bill is a pioneer, an explorer, venturing forth into new territory, unafraid, alone. She hitches up the short skirt of her summer frock to touch the razor in her bloomer pocket. She undoes a fastening at the neck of her frock.

Someone is staring at her neck. She stares back, and the man rises and offers her his seat. She sits with her knees apart, head thrown back. She closes her eyes, dreaming of the white-clad horseman crossing desert sand. She feels an arm pressing against her, a thigh against her thigh, hot breath on her neck. Someone strokes her thigh, runs a hand up and down, slowly. She keeps her eyes shut and dreams of the horseman with the dagger in his belt. She says his name softly and feels the blood beating hard in her throat.

Her mother tells Bill that her father arrived one starless night in the diamond fields in a "ship of the desert." His past did not go beyond that night. She knew nothing about him. He was the first man to ask her to marry him, and she married him because she thought no one else would ask her.

Her mother proclaims her father is a self-made man,

that he made his fortune with the sweat of his brow even though he came from a wealthy family. She says Bill's father is related to the Romanovs or, at any rate, Russian aristocrats. She maintains that a wicked uncle usurped the father's rightful inheritance, that Bill's father's family owned land, miles and miles of birch trees, and horses, that he rode polo ponies as a boy at dawn on the playing fields. But he arrived out here with nothing and made a fortune in the diamond fields, her mother recounts. Then he lost most of it through speculating.

When gold was discovered, everyone was saying, "Gold to lay by and gold to lend, gold to give and gold to spend," and they came rushing up to the Rand in a stagecoach, but now her father spends his days sitting in a dusty office, evaluating other people's diamonds.

It was she, Bill's mother, who inherited the house on R. Street. It is she, Bill's mother, who is related to the right people in the gold town, she tells Bill. "I know everyone who is worth knowing," she tells Bill. Her mother says disdainfully, "Nouveau riche! He started out selling newspapers, you know," speaking of the richest man in the town.

Bill considers her mother has composed a past for her father, created him. Bill wonders whether her father stole the rare diamonds he keeps at the back of his desk.

The house on R. Street is a rambling house, all in bits and pieces. The rooms are dark, shaded by the palms. The garden is large and beautiful, but it has gone wild:

the paths overgrown, the lavender spread into a thick field of mauve, spotted with hovering furry bees. There are patches of bare soil where the hydrangeas have died for want of water. The hibiscus bushes have turned to tangled trees. The grass is weed-choked. The unpruned fruit trees have encroached upon one another's territory. One of the jacarandas, the one at the end of the alley, is so entwined with creeper, it is rotting. The odor of dead flowers mingles with that of the herb bushes that grow by the kitchen door: rosemary, sage, lavender, and the herb her mother soaks for the movement of her bowels.

Afterward, she does not think about what happens to her mother. What she thinks about is her mother's weariness that summer, how weary her mother seemed, how she lay on her back in the darkened room, her mouth slightly open, her arm across her face.

They do not call Bill "fat white woman" anymore. When she walks down the street, they do not call her that anymore. Now they follow her. When she turns toward one of them in the street and quizzes him, he is the one who hesitates. He approaches slowly with a silly smile on his face and a damp gleam of hope in his eye. She looks at his lips, watches them turn dark. Sometimes she bestows a kiss upon him. She does the flutter and probe. When he asks where she learned it, where a girl of her age learned to do something of that sort, she shrugs her shoulders. She whispers in his ear and laughs at his surprise, the flush in the cheek, the flicker of fear in the eyes. She expects all of them to do as she wishes, as everyone always has.

From time to time, her father brings it out. She sees it for the first time in his study after breakfast. The study is on the west side of the house, filled with the rustling sound of the palms. The green shadows shift constantly, and the air smells of her father's cigar, his secrets. There are ashtrays weighted down to the arms of the leather chairs with bags filled with steel balls. Her father moves something across his desk, his fingers like flies, blundering and blowing over the objects there: the paperweight, the felt pad, the clay ink pot, the pen. He opens the drawer of his desk, scratching at the back like a rat. He takes out a steel box, lifts up the lid, shows Bill the diamonds, runs the blunt tips of his fingers across them, caresses them. He lifts one up to the light. It is a large blue-and-white stone, glittering on a gold chain. It is the color of the wings of the angel Bill talks to at the end of her bed. "Let me try it on," she says.

Her father pulls her onto his lap with one arm and presses her against the buttons of his waistcoat. "Bit young for diamonds, don't you think?" He nettles her cheek. She smiles at him, lets him wind his fingers through her glittering hair. "Oh, go on," she says.

He thrusts her from his lap, lays a hand on her shoulder, pushes her over to the mirror on the wall. He loops the pendant around her neck, and the stone shimmers against her skin. He fiddles with the clasp at the nape of her neck.

Bill listens to the uproar in the street, watches the motor-cars shoot by the tram, watches the black victoria follow-ing, led by the black horse.

Bill sits on the sofa in Uncle Charles's room, looking at the shadow on the carpet. She feels as if something is pushing her from behind, something like a hand, pushing her foot down hard on the shadow. All her life, she remembers the flutter underfoot. She feels the fine bones break. The ball of her foot is pressing down hard. She has already crushed it. The back is broken, or the wings.
    There is nothing to do but call the Zulu servant. He holds the bird in the pink shell of his palms. The bird blinks its bronze eyes. The Zulu clucks his tongue and wrings the little neck. "Better like this," he says, and puts the bird back into the cage, its head pressed against the bars.

She thinks of them as Sticking-Out-Ears, or Blue Pull-over, or Pimples. She hardly remembers their faces—rather, just the color of their hair or of their clothes, or just the sound of their shoes. She handles their parts mechanically, as though they were not connected to any-one at all.

. . .

In the bathtub Bill and Haze play a game called Horse. Haze is the horse and Bill the rider, so Bill makes Haze sit between her legs, and they go around the old tub with the feet in the shape of hooves, entwined. They go traveling to foreign countries; they go overseas. Bill is an adventurer, a horseman riding across the desert sands. Bill waves the reins in the air and says, "Faster, faster," and Haze whinnies and tosses her dark head. The water slaps against the sides of the bath, splashes on the tiled floor, spreads like sand.

Bill likes to linger in the dusty streets of the gold town in the hot summer afternoons. The town is racy, with its throbbing vehicles, its gay young women with low-waisted dresses, pointed shoes, and helmet-shaped hats, and with its possibilities. The women laugh. They are bright, familiar, with their glossy lips, their cropped hair, and their light-colored clothes. It is the women who seem illuminated like the famous star of the silent film, the horseman on the white Arab horse. It is the women who have a subtle glow, a halo. The heat brings out the halo. Bill listens to the sound of their laughter lingering in the air. She stares at their clothes.

Bill's father snaps off the lights as he leaves the room. He turns off the dripping tap under the oak tree. He counts out the silver before he pulls out the pounds.

He complains, "I am borrowing from Peter to pay Paul."

Bill's mother says, "I know, I know, I am nothing but a burden on you," and puts her hands to her head.

Bill's father tells Bill, "Diamonds do not grow on trees, you know." He says it was dangerous work digging for diamonds, that the diamond region was a hot, barren region, a place so dry it seemed never to have rained, that there was nothing there but dust and thorn trees and a few wildebeest and fierce light. When it rained, the mist rose in the air, and the Griquas said the place was haunted.

Her father recounts that the diamond mine, the Big Hole, was a vast bowl with smooth sides. So many men crawled up and down the sides of the bowl that it looked black. They swarmed along the sides of the bowl with leaden spades, stirring up a dark cloud of dust. The wires that carried the sand from the bottom of the pit resembled the strings of a harp. They gave off a trembling sound that filled the air. He says you could hear the cries of the diggers who slipped and fell. They died of fever or of smallpox or they simply did not strike "blue ground" soon enough and gave up, or the sand caved in and buried them.

Bill believes that the end to all stories is violent death.

In the evenings on the veranda, her mother mutters about the three old maiden aunts. The twilight makes everything strange, Bill thinks. Bizarre shapes seem to move in the hot darkness. She imagines the three old maids, out there on the hot lawn, weeping in the dark. Her mother speaks of them, shut up in their house in the diamond town. "I never did understand how a father could do such a thing," she says.

Uncle Charles suggests, "Frightened some man would make off with their money, perhaps?"

Bill's mother says, "But to leave them to die like that, three spinsters, shut up in that old house!"

Bill's father says, "They could have married and given up the money."

Bill's mother shakes her head. "No, no, if one married, the others would have been left penniless. He made it impossible for them to marry."

The father says, "But, Temple, they could have found employment of some sort."

Her mother demurs. "Who would have employed them? They couldn't even spell. They could hardly count. Besides, the money would have gone to another branch of the family, to their cousins. The cousins were always sending over suitors, one more handsome than the next."

One of them follows her as she walks alone along the lake. She thinks there is something strange about him, something foreign. She imagines him in the desert, part mirage. He pushes her back against a willow tree. Near the Zoo Lake at twilight, he puts one hand tightly around her throat and with the other he rubs at himself and talks about God.

Uncle Charles maintains religion is a lot of bunkum. He says the Boers are always at it, that they are always going to church and reading the Bible, that they come from afar for *nachtmaal* and pray and sing and preach, and that they all go back home and climb into one big bed and make little Boerlings.

Haze comes pattering past the beds of blue flowers. She holds something in her small plump hand. "Look," she says to Bill.

Bill looks and says, "Ladybird, ladybird, fly away home, your house is on fire, your children are gone," and the ladybird flutters up into the air and then down onto Haze's wrist.

In the evenings, they sit on the veranda and watch the spectacular southern sunsets, the sun falling behind the horizon, the sun bleeding, the sky resplendent.

A delivery wagon passes close to Bill's back, rattling with crates of bottles. Bill curses at the driver. Bill sees a black victoria pulled by a black horse. She hears a dark woman standing in the shadows of an alley calling out to a man. The dark woman with a beret lolls against a wall. A man with a hat drawn down low on his forehead approaches, stands with one hand against the wall. They are face-to-face, whispering urgently, the white man leaning over the dark woman.

Bill is quite sure the Zulu servant would put his head in the fire if her mother asked him to do it. He sleeps on the floor by her bed with his *panga* when the master is away. He makes the fire, cleans, sweeps, washes, polishes, prepares the morning and afternoon tea, cleans the yard, assists with meals. Blind, he finds lost objects for her mother. "John," her mother calls out to him, "have you seen my address book? I cannot see it anywhere."

"Here it is, madame," John says.

He used to serve as coachman before her father bought the motorcar. He sat beside her mother in the victoria with her basket. He served early-morning tea in her mother's bedroom, tapped the spoon against the cup before he entered and drew the curtains to let in the light. He assisted her with her dressing. When he could see, he used to do up the buttons on the back of her dress.

He still draws her bath and buffs her back. He buffs her mother's white back blindly with a sponge in the early mornings, when she lolls in her bath. Bill watches him lean over the bath buffing her mother's back with a sponge, the steam rising about his dark form like a pale bloom.

Bill runs naked down the long hall in the warm dusk to fetch the soap. The servant comes around the corner suddenly, and she runs into him. For a moment, his long, bony body is pressed against hers. She feels the hard, starched uniform, the corned hands. She laughs and turns away quickly, makes her way down the corridor, but not before she sees the ancient Zulu raise his blind gaze with horror.

Look, she is walking through the hot streets of the gold town. She is near the cinema in the powdery air. She sees the fine gold dust catch in the strands of her dark hair. The gold dust slips down the neck of her dress, blows into her eyes. She is staring up at the giant colored poster announcing the film she is going to see, staring at the half-menacing eyes of the horseman, the huge, dark eyes looking out of the famous face under the burnoose. The poster eyes are faded from the sun and the summer storms, but they go on looking down at her from the wall, steadily.

She is staring up into the eyes, as if she were staring at herself, and dreaming of the horseman on his white horse, crossing the desert in a haze of dust. She stares at the horseman, hardly noticing the people who elbow past her, the anonymous throng.

She is jostled by the crowd. Men move dimly around her. She hears the sound of the barefooted black child who bangs against a lamppost with a stick; she hears the beating of hooves against the sand. She is standing on the curb, waiting to cross the street, dreaming, like all the others, her *semblables*, a young girl of fourteen or fifteen in a translucent summer frock and pointed shoes, the dark rope of a plait down her back.

As they sit before the mirror at her mother's dressing table, Bill hears the dawn wind lift with a preliminary murmur. From the horizon a slow, persistent breeze begins to blow. She hears the sound of the luminous wind of morning. The wind blows on with the rising and brightening sun. The dawn sky is swelling with yellow light. It is the brief hour of early morning, before the summer sun rises higher and fills the sky with its brazen glare. A window bangs against the wall, a door rattles. The curtains lift and lull.

From the open casement, Bill feels the wind and the wetness on her face. She watches her mother lift her arm to show her the morning light on the blue hills and a bird's shadow on the wet earth. A bird raises its wings, and the wind lifts it. It veers wildly, flying through the bright white wastes of the dawn. Bill's mother's sleeve flutters against the dead white of her arm as Bill leans toward her.

Her mother is brushing out Bill's hair. Her mother is wearing the silk gown with the loose sleeves, and the sleeve falls away from her arm as she lifts the silver-backed brush. Bill's hair hangs loose and heavy around her shoulders, and the sparks fly.

Before she sees him, she senses someone is there. When Bill looks into the mirror, she can see the doctor has been standing at the door for some time, as he is, not moving. He leans against the jamb of the door and watches them. She notices the flare of his aquiline nostrils, the rosy skin, the close-set eyes.

Bill's mother is as pale as a lily. She shuts herself away in a small, musty room, away from the light, with her secrets, her vials and smelling salts, her herbs, the little smiling Buddha, and the thick amber beads. She does less and less. She hardly moves. Only the tips of her fingers move, and her eyes. She dozes through the days. She lies in the bath, her hair floating about her like weeds on the water. Sometimes Bill sees her staring at the same leaf of a book. The leaves of the book fall about her, yellow and brittle. When Bill picks them up, the edges crumble between her fingers like the wings of moths.

Her mother shrugs. She knows certain passages by heart. She lifts her white chin, quotes in a quavering voice: " 'If music be the food of love, play on.' " She says, " 'Enough, no more. 'Tis not so sweet now as it was before.' "

Bill hears her mother whispering to the woman in the white uniform: "Charles worries me so."

Bill hears the woman say in her hoarse voice, "My dear, what you need is a place away from worry."

Bill's mother says, "Bill worries me to death." The woman clucks her tongue and shakes her head. She fills her mother's glass, and her mother swallows greedily.

. . .

Bill tells Dottie the witch has something in mind. Bill says the witch is making her plans. Dottie asks, "What are you talking about? What plans?"

Bill says, "I know what the witch is going to do when she gets the chance."

Dottie looks at Bill nervously and picks at a spot. She says, "Stop talking nonsense, Bill." She says they ought to speak to their father, that, in her opinion, the best thing to do is to speak to their father and ask him what should be done.

Bill sits opposite their father at dinner and looks into his pale, secretive eyes. She thinks her father looks younger than her mother, and that his blue eyes look as hard as the diamonds he evaluates.

Men would do anything to steal diamonds, her mother declares. They hid them in the hollowed-out pages of books or the barrels of guns. They swallowed them. One man swallowed dozens, her mother maintains. She is not sure of the number, but she is quite sure about the swallowing. She has seen a photograph of the man, staring stupidly into the camera, with the diamonds he swallowed shimmering on a tray beside him.

She explains that the tribesmen who came there to buy guns for their chiefs dug like ants in the vast pit. They dug deeper and deeper in the diamantiferous sand. She says Bill's father did not dig. Her father did not dig in the pit himself but sat, day after day, in the awning of his tent, cross-legged, with his gravel scraper and his fly whisk, sorting through the sand the diggers brought him.

Bill's mother boasts that Bill's father threw the world's largest diamond, the one that was presented to the King, the one that became the Star of Africa, around the office like a ball.

Bill wakes at the sound of her name. The woman in white is leaning over the brass bed, blinking her yellow eyes, calling Bill by her name, the real name, the one no one uses, the one she does not care for. Bill hears her name and the clink of the thermometer against the side of the glass. The woman says, "Open wide the pearly gates," shakes the thermometer with a snap of her plump wrist, and thrusts the thermometer under Bill's tongue.

The woman studies her watch and places two fingers across Bill's wrist. She says that Bill looks flushed, that she looks as though she might be coming down with something, as though she might be feverish. The woman turns the thermometer round and round in the early light, purses her plump dark lips, and says that though Bill has no fever, in her opinion, the doctor should have a little look at Bill.

The cocks crow, answering one another. The flowers in the vase on the bedside table are white and dry.

"It is not conducive to health," Bill hears her father tell the woman in the white uniform. "She needs air," he says. He walks up and down restlessly across the polished parquet floor in the sickroom. His russet hair glints.

The woman says, "Air comes in from everywhere, through all the chinks, and, you know, I always make sure to leave the door open into the corridor, day or night. I hate closed doors."

Bill's father says, "It is not conducive to health to sleep with the windows closed and plants in the room at night. The plants use up all the air."

Everywhere there is a beating, a whirling, a surging. Motorcars flash past her recklessly. Men move toward her, muttering. Young girls in bright dresses brush by her, laughing. There are shouts and voices. A black victoria passes in the street, the cabman flicking up the dark horse. A face glimmers briefly and then is withdrawn. With the afternoon light kindling the bobbed hair of the young girls, bronzing the latticework of the verandas, turning the long leaves of the palms to gold, the city is a place of mystery and promise.

Bill follows a girl in a bright pink dress along a shaded street, making the girl up as she makes her way. The girl is shy but reckless, demure but rash, perhaps, with her bell-shaped hat and her long string of pearls. She has a boyfriend who is a sailor and wears a sailor hat and goes by the name of Markham, Bill is sure. The girl stops, hesitates, crosses the street; Bill follows. They are linked by the light, the leaves above them, the pavement on which they walk.

Bill is an explorer, an adventurer, a horseman, fearless. She will conquer. She will subdue. She is going into new territory, going through the streets of the gold town, going toward the cinema, following and followed in the shimmering heat of the afternoon.

Bill asks the man what is in it for her, but he appears not to have heard. He looks as if he is about to tell her a secret, coming toward her out of the crowd, small bright eyes like a rat's, asking her to model for him. He says he is an artist. All the time he is with her, he maintains he is an artist. All the time she is with him, she eyes the gold fob watch he wears on a chain across his chest.

Her father maintains there was rioting in the mines. He mutters about the *swart gevaar*. He says the police had to fire on the rioters when they asked for the release of a prisoner at the police station. Her father tells Bill that the police shot many dead and wounded many more. He says the rioters threw away their passes, that they dared to attack the police, that the situation was getting out of control. Her father says the women are worse than the men.

On the stairs in the dawn light, Bill sees someone who stops and stares at her fixedly before the figure disappears into the dark.

. . .

The woman in the white uniform stands in the doorway to the sickroom and blocks the faint blue light. She is fairly stout but carries her weight well. She is not beautiful, Bill sees, but she seems to smolder in her white uniform, like ashes, when she wets her thick lips and speaks in her deep, coarse voice and flashes her feral eyes. She smokes cigarettes in the corridor. She takes short sharp puffs and taps the ash onto the carpet.

Bill watches her mother go through French doors into the garden in the moonlight. Heavy cloud sweeps across the moon. Her mother's knees give way beneath her on the lawn. She clings to Bill. Bill holds her and watches the lawn come and go. The garden shivers, and Bill cannot see the house any longer with its red brick, white gables, pergola, creeper-covered walls, rock garden, rare blooms, jacarandas, willows, palms, tangled bushes, and overgrown paths. Only flat darkness lies around her with all the strange quietness of the desert, of the dream places of the earth.

Her mother says, "I would not do it again with any of them."

"Any of them?" Bill asks.

Her mother shakes her head. "No, no, even though your father may be an adequate husband." Her mother adds, "If the truth be known, I am fed up with all of them."

Bill says, "All of them?"

. . .

Bill hears her father mutter as he walks up and down, with his hands behind his back, "Good heavens, one's own relatives are bad enough; one's own wife's relatives are already more than one can stand; one's own wife's half-daft relatives are more than one can endure. One's own flesh and blood is quite enough without these bloody strangers all over the house."

Her mother says, "The nights seem so long and lonely."

Bill slips the hat pin, the one with the pearl on the end, out of the leghorn hat, hides it in her hand, and saunters down the long hallway from her mother's bedroom, into the pale green nursery at the end. She stands under the blades of the fan before the mirror in the sunlight. She becomes aware of her heart suddenly, as though it were pumping not blood but, rather, something thick and sluggish. There is no other sound. Her fingers are stiff. Her legs weak. Her head is spinning.

She is staring at herself in the mirror, throwing back her head, moving her dark eyes dramatically. She likes the shimmer of light in her hair, the clear oval of her face. She likes the curve of her hip, the flat sweep of the stomach, the fist of hair between the thighs. She likes her abject gaze.

She says, "Just look," and unbuttons her blouse. She lifts one arm above her head and then the other, crosses them.

She looks at the gleam in their eyes while they are looking at her. Then she pulls her bloomers slowly down her legs, turns to one side, and lifts her tunic. She shows them her black suspender belt and under it the mark of the elastic. She shows the man who follows her in the street the ladders in her stockings. He loves the ladders. He kneels down, and she lets his lips travel up the ladder from rung to rung. His eyes gleam damply and his breathing grows light.

They look at photographs. They lie on the lounge floor with their stomachs on the carpet in the summer afternoons and turn the pages of the album. The photographs are overexposed, faded, yellow; some are not even pasted in properly, and their edges are curled. Flies buzz about their heads.

"Look, there she is," Haze keeps saying, sucking on the end of her plait. "I am looking," Bill replies, but she thinks the people in the pictures are not as interesting as the ones in the moving pictures she sees in the afternoons.

Her mother gazes out of the photographs from afar, as though she is not looking at anything. Yellow, light-blasted, she sits sulky-mouthed, with a head of dark ringlets, a fringe on her forehead. She sits by a potted palm, or perhaps the palm is only painted in the background, a fake. She sits with her hands folded demurely in her lap. She wears buttoned-up boots, a tucked dress, a wide-brimmed hat with an ostrich feather in the brim. The curved handle of a pale parasol leans against her knee.

. . .

She sees the girl in the water very clearly, but the pulse is drumming in Bill's forehead. The trees sway; the clouds chase one another; the birds swerve together across the sky; the water slaps against the sides of the pool; everything ripples.

Her mother says Uncle Charles is her favorite brother. She says it was she, Bill's mother, who took care of him when he was ill as a child, and he was often ill. It is she who has always taken care of him. Poor Uncle Charles fought in the Boer War and came back badly shellshocked. He heard a shot and fell down and lay flat on the ground, trembling, thinking he was dead.

Bill's father raises his eyebrows and puts a finger to his forehead and twists it and squints at Uncle Charles. Uncle Charles tells Bill he was wounded in the war, that he lost something essential, that they operated on him without anesthesia, that they just cut into him. He knows they removed something essential from his body.

She notices a policeman coming through the crowd with his dark blue helmet. She sees a lady from the Salvation Army who wears a crimson hat, shaking a square red box and singing a hymn.

" 'Abide with me: fast falls the even tide . . . The darkness deepens; Lord, with me abide,' " the woman sings.

. . .

Bill's mother tells her that the priests hold orgies at midnight in the monasteries, that the nuns bury their babies in the backs of convent gardens in the dark of the night, that the nuns are walled up when they sin. Bill can see the nun standing in the dank crypt in a white habit, watching, pale and trembling, reciting her rosary.

Through thin walls, Bill hears her mother sigh, saying, "The doctor says it is a question of rest."

"Rest . . . I wouldn't mind resting at that price!" her father says.

Her mother says, "He says she's the best he could find."

Her father says, "Some find!"

Bill's mother goes on: "The doctor says she will teach me how to rest."

Bill's father says, "What you need is air, Temple. You need exercise. You need to get out of this stifling room. You need to look after your children, who are going to the devil while you are lying here learning how to rest."

Her mother is weeping softly and saying, "I know I'm nothing but a burden on you."

Her father shouts, "For God's sake, you know it's not the expense I'm worrying about."

A bus approaches, stops, settles a moment like a red caravan before it takes off, vanishes in the glare. Bill, too, stops for a moment before a shop window. Something has been torn down and replaced here. In the brash, new city, things are often torn down and replaced. Something is missing.

Behind the plate glass, Bill sees a barefooted man, clothed in black, dressing a mannequin in a shop window. The man, with pins in his mouth, is bending over the mannequin to pin a shirt to its shoulder. The mannequin's severed pink arm lies on the floor. There are several pink arms heaped in a pile. Bill sees her own reflection in the glass and someone else's, like a shadow, beside her. Someone she knows follows Bill through the shadowed streets of the city that has risen from metal found deep in white pyritic rock. They call the place new Nineveh and Babylon.

Bill's mother tells Bill her father is a good man but that from time to time he makes her very unhappy. They have a name for what he does. They call it "marching to Pretoria." Her mother confesses that sometimes in the morning her father just sings the refrain from the song "Marching to Pretoria," and then she knows not to expect him in the evening. Her mother strokes Bill's face and says, "Like most men, I'm afraid, he has a roving eye, you see, Pet."

It is like some old song; she half understands the words. They are shocking but familiar. He tells the same jokes, sings the same songs, and makes up rhymes. He talks about Boers. While the bird pecks at Uncle Charles's hair and chirps, Uncle Charles tells Bill that the Boers are dirty and dishonest, that they are thieves. He says they cannot leave a shop without pocketing something: a knife, a tobacco pipe, or a button. He tells her their houses have dirt floors and his hands stray from his knee to hers. His hands move up and down.

Someone follows her inside the cinema. Some boring man sits behind her as she watches the film, but she pays no attention to him. She is watching the same film again. She is listening to the old lady with the wig who plays the piano. She watches with her eyes half-closed. She follows the film in her head. Like all the rest of the young girls she likes this man, his dusky skin, his menacing eyes, the way he circles around the woman slowly. She knows the circling is for the audience, that all of this is just for them, a game, teasing.

She likes this place, the wideness of the desert, the wildness, the white light. The desert unfurls before her, like a roll of cloth. She disappears into it, rides across the sand to the end of the mind. She breaks away, free.

Bill hears the woman in the white uniform say to her father, "I believe in making people as comfortable as possible."

Bill's father shouts, "This kind of comfort is killing her."

Bill's mother weeps softly among the potted plants.

In the summer afternoons, in the hollow time of day, Bill escapes the shuttered house. She lingers by the lake; she lets men follow her in the deadly heat. She leads them through the speckled shadow of the leafy path to the green bench. She takes them into the thickest shade of the park, to sit there. She stares across the lake at the trees, the bushes, and the water, all of it suffused with the brightness of the hot, still air.

She lets one of them lift her onto his lap. She lets her thin dress slip up her thighs. She lets him hold her small wrist and press this way and that against her cool thigh. She lets him whisper in her ear. She sits on his knees, stares up at the leaves, lazily. She watches the light come down, a coppery haze.

Her mother whispers the word in Bill's ear. Her mother says her father is a "philanderer." Her mother says she sees them when she lies in her bath, when she stares at the pages of her book, when she puts up a hem, when she walks in the garden at dusk, when she sits at the dinner table, when she climbs into bed; she sees her husband's women everywhere she goes. They follow her in her mind, she tells Bill.

They go round and round in the white light. The horseman and the woman are circling and eyeing one another fixedly. Bill looks at the burnoose, the bejeweled dirk, the fancy belt, the riding boots. She imagines the life of a harem. She likes the luxurious tent, the Persian carpets, the cushioned couch.

Bill thinks the woman looks as though she has done

wild and exciting things in the past and will do them again. She likes the woman's white skin, her curls, her bright eyes. Her face looks sad and lovely, Bill thinks. She likes the woman's gentle name, her real name. Bill whispers the woman's name into the dark.

The pastor lifts his gaze, flutters his long eyelashes, and whispers of immortality. He speaks of heaven and the angels there, their wings spread wide in the light, as the organ moans in the shadows of the chapel.

She likes the way the woman struggles virtuously. The woman has only her curving hips, her gestures, the drooping of her eyelids and the crown of light around her head.

Bill likes the dark aristocrat with his gleaming teeth, his flaring nostrils, his occult eyes, his sensuous mouth. She watches the man and the woman part their lips dumbly, as though struggling with something, something more than air. All the while, she listens to the silence, the unspoken words, the imagined words, the words she feels she has heard somewhere else, at the edge of her mind.

The girl in the summer frock comes out of the cinema into the street; she leaves the shadow of the marquee, enters a shop, lingers in the aisles, watches the hands reach avidly for the silks, the shantung, the brocade, the chiffon, the soft crepe, for the velvet, the pure wool, and the cashmere. She gazes at pairs of pink kid gloves with tiny pearl buttons, at fox furs. She sees a gentian blue evening dress with a long net skirt and sequined bodice, and a sleeveless white voile dress with a long waist and a pleated skirt that has slipped from the hanger to the floor. She likes the music, the perfume in the air, the hum of excited voices, the laughter, the confusion. Everyone wants something, many things. At first, all she wants is to touch.

Bill's mother always says, "The right clothes can change your life." Bill wants clothes more elegant than ones that distance her from these women she sees in the street. She wants silk stockings and feathers; she wants linen and chiffon and silk cut by couturiers who know how to show off her curves.

She knows that someone has followed her inside the shop. She knows they are all in love with her, all the boring men. Tightly tucked into their mud-colored suits, the men look thrifty, miserly, worn away with work. They look worried, Bill thinks. Turned inward on their worries, they seem secretive, mysterious, strangers. Their faces seem masked, deathlike.

She moves away from them, sashaying through the aisles of the shop expertly. She is eyeing the merchandise—a pirate. She lifts the skirt of her dress and swoops down and thrusts the gold locket into the pocket of her bloomers.

. . .

Bill slips the gold watch into her pocket as the man who says he is an artist leans close and asks her in his breathy, metallic voice who taught her how to do the flutter and probe.

She walks past a hotel in the gold town. Her mother has pointed out the hotel, told Bill she stayed here with her father when they first came up to the gold town. Her mother has told Bill that Lord Milner held his kindergarten meetings here.

Her mother likes big hotels, likes to say the names of lords and earls. Her mother lifts her pointed chin and waves her white hand and says, "Selborne, Athlone, Milner, Kitchener, Bartle Frere." She tells Bill that one day she will take her overseas to find an English lord. Bill's mother will have nothing less than a lord for her Little Pet. Then Bill will live on an estate in Parktown and ride horses before breakfast and take baths in champagne.

When her mother notices a girl dressed in a tight silk dress, with painted lips and cheeks, she looks at Bill and says, "You ought to put on a little rouge when you go into town in the afternoons, Pet."

Autumn

All her life, she will remember her mother sitting in the flickering desert light, parched lips parted, saying, "Lovely, lovely, never again will I see anything as lovely."

Imagine a high plateau, a thousand miles from the sea. The flat fields lie in the glare of hard light. The sky is a glassy void. The midday sun is hot. It dries the earth until it cracks, and the grass turns dun. There is no rain. The gables of the house are white, the paint bleached and flaking in the arid air. The gate and the gateposts are white.

Look, two forms move across the grass toward the gate. There is a girl who seems to float through the gate in the harsh brightness of the autumn day. Someone follows behind her, like a shadow, but, of course, there are no shadows now. Bill is holding someone by the hand, dragging someone along like a weight as she tries to run to the tram in the dying time of year. As she glances back, she sees someone watching from the window of the house.

They are leaving after luncheon. At luncheon, Bill watches, kicks at the table leg, and waits. The family lingers while the ancient blind servant stumbles in with the serving dishes, banging them down against the mahogany. Baskets of fruit and artificial flowers are mirrored in the high shine of the wood. The woman in the white uniform sits at the top of the table and licks her glossy lips. She gestures with her silver knife to the servant to bring her another mutton chop. She spreads gravy thickly on the mutton chop, the brussels sprouts, and the potato. She pops a hot roast potato into her mouth, bats her plump fingers against her mouth to cool it.

She holds her silver knife the way Bill's father has told Bill not to hold hers. The woman holds the knife as though it were a pencil, her plump pinkie in the air. She points with the knife and complains about the servant. He wears white cotton gloves worn so thin that Bill can see his dark skin. He beats a knife against the gravy boat to get the woman's attention as he offers it to her.

It is warm in the dining room at noon even in the autumn, and the fan continues to beat slowly, stirring up trapped air. The shadow of the fan flickers on the ceiling. Conversation, hardly conversation, comes in little runs. Bill's mother moves her hand in the air vaguely, and her soft sleeve falls away from her arm. She is falling asleep at the table and her small head hangs loose like a wilted flower. The falls of her hair hang like dark petals at the nape of her neck. She slumps at the table. One light leg is crossed over the other. Bill can see the line of her mother's thigh under the thin dress.

Her mother asks the servant to fill her glass. She sips the rosé wine. Bill considers reaching over, lifting the wineglass, and laying her lips where her mother's lips have lain, but before she can, the woman presses her hand on the mother's to stop the mother from saying what she is about to say. The mother moves her dry lips to form a word but stops as the woman presses her hand. Bill's mother pants in silence. Her eyes shimmer white. She moons above the table vacantly. Her face dissolves in the thin air.

The air from the fan makes the white curtains flutter like webs and presses the mother's gray dress against her body. As she rises from the table, Bill can see her mother strain to hold herself erect. She drifts across the floor, like someone floating, an angel. She brushes against the lilies in the crystal bowl on the sideboard, and a bloom falls to the floor.

Bill imagines her father, who is not at the table, sitting in his office, quietly, coolly, staring at uncut stones.

A dry wind is blowing the dust about her. She looks up into the branches of a deadwood tree. The sky is empty. A barefooted black child is playing a penny whistle in the street. The high-pitched notes come to Bill like a scream.

She strides down the street in the school uniform, the long-sleeved shirt, the green tie, the green tunic with the round neck, the green felt hat with the band around the rim, the thick black stockings. She holds a brown paper packet firmly with one hand and her mother anchored with the other. Bill sails onward. She tows her mother in the dust of her wake. Her mother drags on Bill's arm. Her mother tries to hold back, complaining about the bright light.

In the autumn afternoon, the garden is very still. The roses have rotted, the petals dropped to the ground, heavy with scent. The delphiniums, the sweet williams, the Canterbury bells, the agapanthi have faded and died for want of water. Bare branches web the sky. Gray birds drift together and land on them like gray leaves. The sun is a blanched yellow in a white sky. Bill's lips are dry, her elbows rough, her hair puffed around her face in the electric air. In her mother's dark hair, little points of light shine like fire.

Her mother stands very still in the muted garden. She unfurls her faded parasol and turns her head from side to side among the jacarandas and the golden oaks and the palms. With her eyes half-closed in the cool shadow, she breathes the air in little gulps like water.

Bill hears the sound of a voice shouting loudly in the house, the deep man's voice of the woman in the white uniform shouting loudly on the telephone. As Bill strides through the garden, trailing her mother behind her, Bill sees the woman in the white uniform looking through the lounge window. Her eyes gleam gold.

The autumn days are warm and the nights are as cold and windy as in the desert. The three sisters sit up at night, sequestered, to sew. They crouch by the lamp in the cold room under the corrugated iron roof and sew until they are purblind. Bill lifts her eyes from her needle and stares up into the vast sky. She looks for shooting stars. The sky is filled with stars like ice. Bill sees a star fall and fall, melting in the liquid blackness of the southern sky.

When the woman in the white uniform asks why Bill is not preparing for school, she walks through the bedroom, toward her father's dressing room. The woman catches

Bill's hand and says, "Just look at you. You can't go to school like that, half-naked. Here." Bill turns her hand back and forth impatiently while the woman slowly buttons up the cuffs of Bill's long-sleeved shirt, the woman's hot fingers fluttering at Bill's wrists, caressingly. "You'll worry your mother to death!" the woman says as Bill breaks away. The woman, Bill knows, stands outside the dressing-room door like a sentinel.

It is hot and airless in the dressing room. There are no windows. Bill goes through the shallow drawers, unfolding the long silk socks, folded tightly, one inside the other, like colored eggs. She hunts between the rainbow-colored shirts, the white initialed handkerchiefs, the ironed underwear. She opens the tall armoire against the wall and plunges her hand into the pockets of jackets, waistcoats, trousers, the cashmere coat. She breathes in the musty odor of buried things.

But she finds nothing: no money, not even the stub of a ticket from the cinema. Her father does not care for the cinema. Her father looks at her with his still blue eyes and says he would not be caught dead there.

Bill kneels down and feels around blindly. She thrusts her fingers into the toes of her father's shiny shoes. On her knees as though praying, she finds what she is after. She finds the bottle with the *tickies*. She empties it and fills her broad palms with her father's silver coins. There are so many of them that they slip through her fingers to the floor.

. . .

Bill follows her mother onto the empty lawn in the moonlight. Bill watches the moon slipping through cloud, escaping across the sky. The marks of the moon are on her mother, on the curve of her neck, her skin. Her face is pale; there is a silver glimmer in her transparent eyes. She walks unsteadily in her narrow shoes. She stumbles. Bill tries to hold on to her, but her mother's dress is slippery, and she slips from Bill's arms.

The house gleams behind them, ghostlike, the gables silver. The smoke from the servants' fire blows blue. The trees, the grass, the garden tap, all fade. At this late-evening hour, the garden is sinking fast into darkness.

They stagger on in the moonlight. The mother's head slumps forward, and her whole body is slack. She casts an arm about Bill's neck. The tears spill from her eyes, and she moans, "Everything is slipping through my fingers, everything."

Like a swimmer, she is sinking. Her hand is slipping out of Bill's. Then her mother is lying silently before Bill on the grass. Her mother has plunged from a great height. She has come down. She remains curled on the grass, her silver dress crushed between her legs, her head back, her hair spread out beneath her. She has departed. The witch has got her.

Uncle Charles whispers in the half-dark of the back bedroom. He tells her the one about Oom Paul in England.

He says Oom Paul was a cowherd, that when he went to England he kept spitting on the marble floor of Buckingham Palace. The servant with the silver spittoon rushed back and forth. Paul Kruger kept on spitting on the floor. Paul Kruger said, "Get out of the way, man," but the servant kept rushing backward and forward, offering the spittoon, diligently. Finally, Paul Kruger shouted, "Get out of the way, man, or I'll spit in that damn thing!"

Sometimes the wind blows so hard in the night, Bill can hear nothing else. Sometimes she hears the front door close quietly and someone enter or someone leave the house.

Bill sits beside her mother, who slumps in the armchair in the blue light of the sickroom. It is the time of year when the evening star shines low in the blue night sky. Bill watches her mother sip from her glass and read, a mauve shawl draped around her shoulders. Her mother reads in the blue light, staring at the same page. When the wind blows, the yellow pages flutter back and forth.

Bill thinks her mother is grieving over the three aunts, dead in the diamond town, their virginity bound by their father's will, and the sister, Maud, driven by a jealous husband into a tree, her ankles and wrists snapped against the dashboard, or, perhaps, she is just listening to the dead leaves falling outside the window like the notes of a scale tumbling down a line of music.

. . .

Haze practices scales, arpeggios, trills, in the blue shadows of the autumn afternoons. She plays the same ones again and again. Her hands wander back and forth desultorily through the white desert of the keys.

Bill stands on the steps in her boots, her hands on her hips, and scowls. Haze meets her gaze and very deliberately, holding the damper pedal down hard, she begins to play the heavy chords of a sonata.

Bill is waiting for the tram outside the house on R. Street. The palms sway brightly in the autumn glare like palms in an oasis of the mind. The house shimmers behind them, hardly a house, more a monument, a tombstone.

Her mother stands beside her. Bill thinks her mother looks smaller in the light of the early afternoon. She looks out of focus, like the mother in the photographs. She is melting like wax in the sun. Her skin is whiter than wax. She holds the faded parasol to shade her white skin. Her umber hair falls all over her face, and her chiffon dress is creased. She rubs her pale eyes and sways back and forth.

Bill draws her along ruthlessly, waving in the air the brown paper packet tied with the string.

Bill's mother frets, "What about my medicine, Pet?"

Bill says flatly, "You are not going to need medicine where we are going. Come on, now, we have to hurry."

She just gives them a look, and they follow her by the lake while twilight dissolves in bright gleams in the dry branches. A bird sings and is silent. There is a lingering smell of sweetness and decay. Motes of dust fall from the air. The sweeping beams of mellow light touch the tips of the trees. In the liquid shadow of the willow tree, one of them asks her for a kiss. She stirs beside him on the bench, gazes at the sun-filled water of the lake. The lake shimmers in the cool evening light. The willows hang low over the still water of the lake and cluster on the artificial island near the other side.

He speaks in such a quiet voice, she can hardly hear what he is saying. His clothes look expensive: the double-breasted suit is linen; the tie is silk. The man lifts his hand toward her face, and she notices the diamond ring in its thick gold setting. The diamond flings spangles in her eyes. "And then?" he says, slipping it from his finger.

"That will do for now," she commands.

Bill stands under the fan in the nursery. The blades of the fan whirl and pulse above her unsteadily, following one another around and around, a blur of blades, a moth's wings. She lifts her skirt and slips her bloomers down her legs. She uses the sharp end of the pearl-tipped hat pin. She pushes hard with the pin. She pushes the pin into the fist of hair between the thighs. She moans softly. Her head spins.

Good! Good! Better like that. Clean.

She feels herself drawing away from the pain. She watches her hand lift and fall curiously in the mirror, moving of its own accord, like a fly buzzing, hovering, landing, preening itself. She sees the trickling red. In the mirror, she sees someone else's face, a face in a film. She sees the downcast gaze.

It is the fading time of year. The sky turns an iron blue, the wind blows the dust up in the air, and the nights shine starlit and cool. It is the time of year when they burn the grass, and blue smoke lingers in the air. The women sit with shawls around their shoulders on the glassed-in veranda in the morning sun and sew, sipping endless cups of steaming tea from transparent china cups. They talk about their bodies, how dry their hair has become—like straw, my dear; Bill's mother sighs and lifts the tips of her fingers to trace an eyebrow that arches thinly like the wing of a bird. They talk about the sag and fall of their breasts, about their immovable bowels. They use mysterious, familiar words. So-and-so did not keep her legs crossed, I am afraid, my dear, and now she has a bun in the oven. So-and-so—and they stare at Bill—thinks she is the bee's knees.

In the street, Bill hears the sound of the wind, the crack of the branches, the voice of the woman talking on the telephone, and, louder than anything else, Bill hears the sound of the white horse ridden by the horseman thudding across the sand.

Shards of light stab her eyes as she watches the girl swim. Through the glare, Bill is watching the older girl, the broad-shouldered one with the silky fair hair, the white teeth, and the slow smile. The girl is swimming backstroke up and down the pool in her thin black racing costume, reaching back her arms and lifting her shoulders out of the water so that Bill can see her broad shoulders, her firm breasts, her flat stomach, and the bones of her hips through the spray. The girl is arching her back for Bill to see.

The girl keeps going up and down, the water splashing the green plastic cap with the strap under the chin, the eyes. No one else is watching. Everyone has left the pool. Everyone is changing except for Bill. The girl, too, stops kicking, as though she has read Bill's mind, has decided to do something else, something more exciting.

Bill, Dottie, and Haze stand on the lawn under the glassy brightness of the sky. Dust blows about them, and the wind moans in the bamboo shoots. Bill asks Dottie, "Have you seen Haze?"

Haze says, "Here I am," and pulls on her dark plait.

Dottie scans the horizon and says, "Where *has* Haze gone?"

Haze shouts, "I am here. I am here," and stamps her small plump foot in dry grass. Dottie turns her head back and forth. She says to Bill, "How very strange. I have looked everywhere. Haze seems to have disappeared."

Haze pulls at the red ribbon in her plait and sputters, "I am here. I am here."

Bill shades her eyes from the sun and says, "She must be down in the garden, picking her nose."

. . .

Bill finds the shiny pink ones, the dull gray ones, the bone-colored ones, the thin ones, the fat ones, the curved ones for socks. The knitting needles are all hidden under the paper in the bottom drawer of the dresser in the small room where the woman in the white uniform now sleeps.

The woman steals Bill's mother's French soap and leaves it in the bath, steals her mother's brittle blue writing paper and hides it under the mattress. The woman steals her mother's knitting needles. Bill puts the knitting needles back in her mother's flowered knitting bag.

Her mother's face shimmers in the moonlight. She lies on her back beside Bill on the lawn, hands at her sides, hair spread around her, like someone floating on water. She stares up into the empty blue waves of the night sky.

She tells Bill that she feels she is drowning in an underground sea, and that she prefers to be far away from people, that she has come to the conclusion that people, even the good ones, take advantage of you, that they cannot help it, it is their nature. What they really want is a servant, someone to listen when they talk, someone to tell them what they want to hear—that they can live forever. As for the bad ones, her mother says that they are vultures, picking over the flesh of the dying and the dead.

Bill sits beside her mother on the grass and stares at the damp face of the moon and at the dead blooms. She looks into the distance at the bitter sweep of the veld where it dips away into the valley.

Bill catches sight of the woman in the white uniform on the telephone, shouting excitedly. Bill points toward the street, though she cannot yet see the tram coming. Her mother is shading her eyes from the sun, blinking blindly into the golden leaves of a tree. It looks like a tree in heaven, Bill thinks. Her mother is looking at the small dun birds rising and falling, lost souls caught in the leaves that hang down like golden bats. She is moving her lips, muttering something to herself.

Bill implores her mother to hurry. Bill holds her mother by the wrist and drags her onward through the gate, through rustling leaves. Bill glances over her shoulder and sees the woman in the white uniform looking through the window.

Bill never tells them the name of the one who taught her how to do it. She never says anything about the older girl, the captain of the swimming team, the one in the class above her, who swam in the thin racing costume and the green cap with the strap under her chin, the one who emerged from the water, her skin luminous, bepearled, the one they laid out on the dry grass.

Bill leads one of them along the edge of the lake in the dusky light. She takes him into a grove of birch. The white bark glistens in the cool dusk. While she handles his life, she watches a duck swim away slowly across the water, dipping his dark glittering head. While he dies in her hands, she sees the sun fall below the horizon, bleeding across the sky.

She hears the sound of the tram in the distance. She sees the sparks fly from the electric tracks. She lets her breath out. Her heart is quickening. She has the packet firmly grasped in one hand and her mother's wrist in the other. She draws her mother onward, holds her firmly, ruthlessly. The shadow of the parasol flows across her mother's face as she moves.

Bill is not sure what she will do with her mother when she arrives; she is not sure what she will do with the packet, either.

When Bill complains of the stomachache and lies down on the bed in the sickroom beside her mother with a wet handkerchief over her eyes, the woman in the white uniform strokes Bill's forehead with her plump fingers and says maybe the doctor should take a little look.

He comes slowly across the room, over to the bed, and sits down. His scent disturbs the air. Beneath the soap scent, Bill detects a darker one. He takes Bill's pulse, glancing at her mother on the other side of the bed. Her mother's eyes shimmer in the muted light. The doctor's face glows rosily; the close-set eyes dart back and forth;

his Cupid's bow mouth moves. His clean, plump hands hop over Bill's body. She thinks his hands look like toads hopping across her chest. She can hear his heavy breathing.

Her mother moves her thin lips as the doctor speaks, as though it were she and not Bill whom the doctor is addressing. Bill's mother lies on the bed among the wilting plants, moving her hands to her hair, her eyes. She tells Bill to shut her eyes, to lie quite still, to feel the cool of the stethoscope, the soothing hands.

Bill watches the objects disappear into darkness: the basin, the towel horse, the big armoire that crouches in a corner of the nursery. The day is dropping from her slowly as she watches.

Bill lies between Dottie and Haze, propped up high on dim white pillows, staring out through the bay window, searching for the light of the witch. Bill says that the witch is coming for their mother, just watch. Dottie shivers and pulls the blankets around her narrow shoulders. She says, "Don't say such an awful thing, Bill."

"Will the witch take Mummy away?" Haze asks.

"Yes, far away from this place," Bill answers.

"Won't Father stop the witch?" Haze inquires.

Bill tells her, "There is nothing he can do."

Dottie says, "I am going to ask him to do something."

In the dry autumn months, the clouds gather and roll across the sky, heavy as rocks. When the lights are out,

Bill goes to the bay window in her nightgown and opens the shutters onto the garden. She listens to the thunder booming in the distance and hears the horseman riding across the sand. In the profound darkness, Bill can hear the dull booming and thudding of the horse's hooves as her phantom horseman thunders through the night.

She sees it approaching in the distance. The tram hangs suspended in the middle distance, caught in the white light, a caravan of the desert. It hangs there, shimmering. Then it plunges on, drawing closer until she can hear the sound of it, the yaw and the clatter of the tram.

She has often seen him weep, Bill's mother tells her. Her father cannot bear the sight of a sick child or a wounded animal, her mother says. He never forgets a birthday or an anniversary. He is a good man, her mother maintains, when you get right down to it. Fundamentally, he is a good man, her mother assures Bill. Her mother says that the irony is that she was not in love with him, that she married him because she thought no one else would ask her, that he wore her down, wore her out, carried her off. He called her "Kitty" for her soft eyes back then.

On the walls, there are also paintings by the maiden aunt who died shut up in the house in the diamond town, holding on to her inheritance, despite the suitors sent over by the rival branch of the family. There is one of twin towers with the lovers at the top of each of them, leaning toward one another, their thin arms outstretched, their hands never quite touching against a blue sky. There is one of a drunken man, his overturned glass at his side, his head on his hand, who stares at the woman with snakes for hair, and the one that is Bill's favorite, of the lovely woman who sits in an open window, one shoulder higher than the other, goblins hiding in the leaves of the tree and in the sea below, called *Charmed Magic Casements*.

She never forgets that. She never forgets what happens to her mother, but she chests her cards. She never tells anyone about any of it, not even about the cloakroom.

Afterward, she locks herself in the cloakroom with the stained basin, the green raincoats, the galoshes. In the autumn it is as dark and as cold as a vault. The air is musty from being long enclosed.

It was in there that Uncle Charles told her the one about the tram and the father who turns into strawberry jam.

From the cloakroom, she hears voices in the hall. She opens the door a crack and sees her father stride away from the china cabinet, the shell-shaped cups and saucers shaking on the shelves. He has his hands in his russet hair as he sits down heavily on the kist beside the dusty proteas. He is saying, "But she cannot have disappeared! People do not just disappear!"

The policeman stands at the foot of the stairs, his hat in his hand. He says, "I am afraid women do disappear all the time, sir. Sometimes it is because they wish to disappear. Perhaps she has gone on a voyage of some sort, sir."

Now they whistle when she sashays down the street in the hard light of the autumn afternoons. She paints her lips. She paints her cheeks. She dabs scent, the one called magic in French, on the tip of her tongue. She swings her hips. She stares back at them brazenly. She holds them with her gaze. She makes them walk toward her. Their eyes gleam and their lips part.

One of them offers her a cigarette from a gold case. She refuses the cigarette but fingers the case. His dark downcast eyes follow the curves of her body, touch her hair, her lips, the buttons of her blouse, her thighs, her thighs.

After breakfast every morning, she carries her empty turned-over eggshell in its eggcup and enters the dark study, where her father sits at the desk with the green lamp, reading old copies of *The Diamond Times* and smoking thin cigars in his silk dressing gown. The light flickers, shadows barb the carpet, and the palms hiss in the wind. She tiptoes across the worn carpet and offers her father the empty eggshell. He waves his hands and thanks her for the special gift. She watches his hands, the faded freckles, the gold hair, the slow movements, as he lifts the spoon aloft and cracks open the empty eggshell with a flourish. Then, ever surprised, he exclaims, "But there's nothing inside!"

Bill puts one arm around her mother's waist and the other under her knees and lifts her like a bride onto the back of the tram. Her mother's fingers claw at Bill's neck. Her body flutters as the tram lurches. The parasol clatters to the floor. Bill falls heavily onto the seat with her mother in her lap. They fall together, entwined. Her mother's breasts press against Bill's breasts; her damp hair is in Bill's mouth and eyes. Her mother's forehead shines. Sweat circles the armpits of her gray dress. Her mother is sinking into Bill, seeping into her. Her mother's eyes are deep hollows. Her skin is as pale as clay. Her mother oozes into Bill's flesh.

The dust rises around them as the tram clatters down the street. Bill hears the sound of the tram and behind the tram the sad clippedy-clop of horse's hooves. Bill sees the shadows flow across the back of the black horse.

It was Uncle Charles's favorite, blue-green and glittering, the one that flitted gracefully, hopped, stiff tail aloft, onto her shoulder, and pecked at her cheek, saying, "Coca-Cola, Coca-Cola." She walked through the darkened rooms of the shuttered house with him on her shoulder. It was his backbone she crushed with her foot. She remembers the flutter underfoot and the tall Zulu, his head bowed, looking down at the crushed bird in the pink palm of his hand.

Sometimes all she has to do is to show them her hair. They do what she wants them to do when she shows them her hair. They sit on the bench in the greenest part of the park and stare at her gleaming hair. One of them begs her to let down her hair. Swift shadows flit across the water, past her face. She says, "Like Rapunzel?" She takes off her school hat. She undoes the string at the end of the plait, unwinds it, spreads the thick hair slowly around her shoulders and across her face. Veiled, she looks out at the green shade. He blinks as though sunstruck.

A bee drifts down and hums around their heads. Haze and Bill lie head-to-head on their stomachs in the burnt grass under the midday sun. They lift their chins, stretch their necks, and reach with their tongues. They touch the tips of their pink tongues together. They giggle and roll around in the grass, and the bee stings Haze's arm. Dottie says, "That's what happens when you two act like idiots."

What Bill likes to do in the autumn afternoons is to walk in the streets of the town. The streets run gold in the sunlight. The pavements are illuminated. She yields to the fine flush of a face, the bright crown of light in the hair. She watches one of them approaching, the soft clothes clinging, the light footsteps rising in the air. The girl walks past Bill, her dress brushing against her. Bill turns and follows her. The wind is blowing the girl's dress against her legs. She walks across the fissured pavement, her head held high. The girl slows down slightly to shift the collar of her dress, to adjust a strap, to glance behind her. She stops, leans against a wall, snaps open her compact in the shade, pats her nose with a fluffy pink powder puff. She turns and stares at Bill.

Bill watches the girl move first in one direction, then in another, as though she were lost, as though one way were as good as another. She stumbles, rubs her brittle ankle, slows her steps to a halt. She hesitates and glances over her shoulder. Bill follows her inside a hotel. Bill hears the tap-tap of her high-heeled shoes as the girl goes up the red polished steps. Bill follows.

She thinks that people are not like walled fortresses but, rather, like tents whose flaps you can just lift up when you want to enter and rummage around.

In silence, Dottie and Bill leave the nursery in their hats and white gloves. They slip down the dim stairs and through the white garden gate to take the tram into the gold town. They sit side by side in the smoky air outside the office on a horsehair settee, leaning over, reading a magazine. Dottie licks a trembling finger to turn the page. When they enter the office, the sunlight flows through the blinds and lies in dusty pools on the parquet floor.

Bill slumps opposite her father in the deep shadows of a shabby armchair. She crosses her legs, sees the sunlight on her boots. The sunlight makes the boots look wavy, weak, broken. Bill feels Dottie's body flutter, perched on the arm of the chair beside Bill.

Their father looks up, blinking his calm, still eyes. Bill watches his wooden face, his obtuse eyes. "Well, fire away, fire away," her father urges Dottie.

Her mother sits in the sickroom among the plants that are wilting from too little air and too much water. She tells Bill, "The trees flashed; the lamppost flew up in a shower. There must have been a thudding in her ears as the motorcar smashed into the tree." Her mother puts her hands to her head and adds, "Pet, they are killing me, too, more slowly, but killing me just the same."

The man with the greasy hair follows her near the Zoo Lake. The water is the color of red mud and foams slightly yellow at the edges. Great bearded trees touch its surface. In the distance, the scattered suburbs show lights. The shadows of high palms fall like black fingers in the dust. He comes toward her in the stream of gold light and dust. He has his hand around her neck. She struggles, gasping for breath. The air is going from her; the light is dimming. She is going to die like this. They will find her body floating facedown in the water among the weeds. He holds her with one hand and with the other he unbuttons himself and rubs himself and talks about God the Father, God the Son, and God the Holy Ghost. She remembers something a girl told her at school. She kicks him hard. He bends over low, swearing bloody hell.

When she sees the bruises on Bill's neck, her mother tells Bill to turn up the collar of her shirt. "You wouldn't want anyone to see, now, would you, Pet?" she says.

Uncle Charles tells Bill the one about the nanny goat: "The night was dark and stormy; the nanny goat was blind. She jumped into a barbed-wire fence and scratched her never-you-mind."

The termites have made a house under the drooping branches of a tree. The Zulu points out the dark passages that lead from the house to the trunk.

He says the termites make dark passages because they do not like the light.

The woman wears a blue cape over her uniform in the cool evenings. She wears a diamond brooch in the form of a bow on her breast. The woman has large breasts, wide hips, and plump thighs in white stockings. Her stockings rustle mysteriously as her plump thighs brush together as she hurries down the corridor. Bill watches her disappearing down the dim corridor with something in her hand. Bill follows the woman under the portrait of Lord Milner, past the potted palms that stand silently like leafy sentries outside the sickroom. Bill stands beside the potted palms at the closed door. She hears the woman say, "Out for the count."

The doctor says, "That's the way I like them."

Bill tries to hold her mother upright, but her head keeps rolling onto Bill's shoulder. Her mother shades her eyes with her hand, gasps, "I feel so dizzy, Pet."

Bill says, "Hold on to me," but her mother is not holding on to anything; her mother is slipping from the worn leather seat as the tram turns a corner. Bill holds on to her mother's waist, tightly. She holds her mother with her arms, with her gaze. She flashes her eyes menacingly. Bill holds on to her mother and the brown paper package. She uses it to fan a fly from her mother's damp face.

Her mother struggles with Bill. Her mother twists on the seat, moaning, mumbling about her handkerchief, her hat, her handbag, her medicine, attempting to rise. Bill holds on to her mother tightly, stubbornly, as the tram rattles onward down the street. The tram shrieks through the streets of the gold town.

The streets are hard and burnished by the sun. They churn with the wheels of motorcars and lorries and victorias. A black victoria follows close behind them. Bill hears the sad sound of the horse's hooves and the rattling of the tram. A motorcar shoots by them, backfiring like the crack of a gun. The noises rise in the air.

Her mother mumbles, like a small child, Bill thinks, "Where are you taking me to, Pet? What are we going to do?" Her mother says, "You know I need to rest in the afternoons. You know I need to lie down in the dark in the afternoons."

The servants are growing sullen. Bill does not hear their easy laughter coming from their courtyard any longer. She hears only the cluck of doomed chickens, scratching in the dust. The ancient Zulu sits on a bench and stares impassively at the mote-flecked sunlight. His shoulders slump, so that he seems narrower. Glasses slip through his bony fingers and shatter on the floor. Dust gathers.

The woman in the white uniform says she found the Zulu standing beside her bed in the night. She says he should be sent back to the location where the nanny's twins have already been sent.

The Zulu does not scare. He complains that the recipe the woman gave him for the syrup on the ice cream stuck to the cut glass. He could not wash it clean, though he scrubbed at it for hours. Also, he says he found the hot-water tap left running on a large cucumber in the woman's bathroom. He lets the soufflé tumble down the back of the woman in the white uniform. He retreats to his windowless room and lies on his bed, his feet against the door, smoking his pipe. When Bill goes to find him, she smells smoke and sour sweat and malady seeping through the crack under his door.

The servants shiver and stretch the bare fingers of gloved hands over the coal fire in the courtyard in the cold nights. They close their windows and put newspaper under the doors and into the cracks in the walls to keep out the cold. They bring coals inside their rooms, and one of them dies from the fumes.

Bill's mother says that natives have absolutely no idea of time. When the Zulu takes his holiday, her mother says she has no idea when he will come back. When he does, Bill watches from the window on the staircase as he shuffles up the driveway with a brown paper packet under his arm, his head bowed, his face gray. His toes stick out of the sides of his *tackies*. Her mother says he has come back a bag of bones. The Zulu tells Bill they have poisoned all his children, that all his little ones are dead. "Jealousy," he says, when Bill asks why.

He no longer sings out at dawn in his deep bass voice as he piles the furniture up in the middle of the lounge to polish the floor.

The parson stands in the pulpit and tells them not to lay up treasures for themselves on earth, where moth and rust do corrupt, and thieves break in and steal.

They are riding together, riding the tram. Back and forth they sway with the movement of the tram. Up and down goes the tram itself through the streets of the town. Laced together, they look out at the streets rushing by, at the heads bobbing, the lace curtains fluttering, the polished steps gleaming in the high light. People wander and watch. Everyone is looking for something. They are like wanderers in the desert looking for an oasis, Bill thinks.

Perched on high, Bill holds on to her mother and points out of the window of the tram at the tin roofs of the houses glinting white under the autumn sky, the dust blowing up into the branches of the blue gum trees. She shows her mother the pale moon and the white sun in the sky. Her mother throws back her head and moves her eyes and parts her lips, but nothing comes from her lips now.

Bill lies on the bed in the sickroom next to her mother and watches the toads descend toward the wound. The doctor looks Bill in the eye and apologizes for what he must do. Bill sits up, seizes his hand in hers, and bites it hard. He gives off a little gasp. Her mother moans, "It only takes a moment, Pet."

Her mother lies floating for hours in the bath. She bathes in the morning and then again in the evening after she rises from her rest. She lies in hot water, the steam rising around her, her dark hair floating on the surface of the water like weeds. She emerges from the water panting, trembling, the water flowing from her white skin in silver streams. The woman in the white uniform calls Bill's mother Lily because of her white skin.

Bill stands against the basin and watches the woman soap the flannel with the French soap. The woman passes the flannel across the folds of Bill's mother's white skin, offers it to her. She shrugs her shoulders and lies back in the water, lifts her hips, and the woman plunges her arm into the water and scrubs between Bill's mother's legs. As the woman scrubs, she glances over her shoulder and raises her thick eyebrows at Bill. Bill's mother laughs. She says, "She is only a baby."

The woman says, "Tell her not to stare."

The woman in the white uniform swells and ripens. She sits up at night by Bill's mother's bed with her back propped against the wall and eats chocolate biscuits. The woman licks the chocolate from her lips. Crumbs fleck her white uniform. When she sees Bill watching her from the doorway, the woman lifts a thick eyebrow. She puts a finger to her pursed lips.

She lingers in the corridor outside the nursery at night, smoking Bill's mother's Craven A cigarettes, picking at her big uneven teeth, and whispering to the doctor. A fly drones around the woman's head. There are cigarette burns on the dresser beside her bed, and the mirror above the dressing table is cracked.

Bill hears her mother say sadly, "The doctor says she is necessary."

Her father says gently, "If you think it will help, Temple."

Her mother says, "The doctor says I cannot do without her help."

Her father says, "I will do whatever you think will help, Temple."

Her father's face is ruddy. The back of his neck is ruddy. He looks sturdy, solid, healthy. His shoulders are square. His mustache is stiff as straw. His eyes are a cool blue. He tells Dottie there is no need for the water-works, but Bill sees her father bury his face in his arms and weep.

Her mother says, "Not a good lover, actually, to tell you the truth, I could see it from the start. He was too eager at the beginning. Once he made me do it in the back of a taxi, can you imagine? Then later, he just lost interest altogether. Can't imagine why."

Below the table in the dim light, Bill sees the plump knee pressed against the gray, and the hand holding the thigh.

Bill sees a silver glove, a face, the glint of white hair; then the cabman flicks up the horse, and the face is withdrawn under the hood. Bill imagines the doctor following with a silver blanket over his plump knees, the doctor coming to get them, coming to steal her mother like a bandit on a black horse.

Bill hears someone walking in the corridor in the middle of the night, lingering there. She hears low voices. She hears a chuckle and a moan.

. . .

The woman in the white uniform leaves the bathwater with the soap in it in the bath. Bill sees the French soap there, stuck to the bottom of the bath, green and soft around the edges, melting slowly. Bill hears the woman talking on the telephone in the hall. She is ordering from the list she holds in her hand. The woman says, "I told you to send three cakes of the French soap. Yes, yes, that is the kind of soap madame requires, the French soap. Did you get that? I said FRENCH."

Bill places her hands on her mother's shoulders and pulls at her. Bill sits astride her mother's legs and tries to lift her shoulders from the dark earth. In the dark, her face is white as marble. She lies in the darkest part of the garden, in black space. She seems about to rise from the stiff grass, but she falls back and remains still. The wind laps at the hem of her dress and seeps around her legs.

Bill sees someone else lying there gazing up blindly at the night sky. Her mother has dissolved, volatilized. The witch has snatched her up. Her garden, too, has vanished. Bill stands in someone else's garden, a silent and mysterious place. She is lost in a garden that she has given away.

Sometimes Bill hears her mother murmuring in her sleep as she lies on the bed in the muted light of the shuttered sickroom, as though her mother were murmuring to a lover, murmuring a dark and passionate secret.

Bill stands at the door to her mother's room and sings "Beautiful Dreamer, wake unto me," but her mother does not wake.

The woman murmurs to Bill, "My dear, I wish only to be your friend. You don't understand how responsible I feel for you until something more suitable can be arranged."

"Suitable?" Bill says.

The woman says, "You don't understand the tremendous interest I take in you."

Bill says, "Oh, but I do, you know, I do."

Bill's mother says, "When I die, you'd better come quickly, Pet, before they rip the rings from my fingers."

Bill and Dottie hold Haze down among the aloes and make her drink the bitter juice from the aloe leaf. When she screams, they tell her to shut up, and they drag her into the privy for punishment and thrust her head down the hole and pull the chain.

The token of gratitude varies. Certain fancy caresses, certain slow shiftings, certain magic made with the soft mouth draw a handsome remuneration. Bill acquires a gold watch with an inscription to someone's wife, jade in the shape of a cross, a locket in the shape of a heart with a photograph of someone unknown, the light in her hair like a bright crown behind her head.

A bird shatters a pane in an upstairs window of the house. No one replaces the pane despite the draft.

Bill thinks her mother, lying in the grass, would probably not dare to weep in this way except with Bill. She turns to the weeping woman on the grass in the moonlight and slaps her face hard. Bill slaps her mother on the cheek. Her mother raises herself, stares at Bill, blinks. Then her mother puts Bill's hand to the mark on her cheek.

Bill rises from the grass in the moonlight, detaches a clinging twig with slow care from her mother's skirt, and lifts her to her feet. Bill stands with her mother in the light of the moon on the lawn. Her mother does not move. She seems to wait for something. Bill wonders what she is waiting for. They gaze at one another in the moon-blanched light.

Bill watches the girl sinking down through the sun-filled water of the swimming pool. Bill does not move, the light too bright, the blood too quick in her temples, the sun holding her back like a hand, the sweat dripping down from her forehead, down, down her face.

What Uncle Charles says about the Boers is that they have massacred the Bible. They have turned "Gird up

your loins" into *"Maak vas jou broek."* They have massacred Shakespeare; they have turned "I am your father's
ghost" into *"Ek is jou papa se spoek."*

Uncle Charles says that the Boers are a violent people
who beat their natives with *shamboks,* who beat their
wives, their children, that if they do not like their wives,
they take them out behind the barn and get rid of them.

She is standing on the curb watching the new traffic lights
blink slowly from red to green. The taxicabs honk their
horns. A long black hearselike motorcar with a silver fairy
on its bonnet flies by. A man is playing an accordion on the
corner, pumping and swinging his hands, singing, " 'No,
we have no bananas, we have no bananas today.' "

The city is heaving and surging around them. Bill can
hear the shuffle and stamp of feet. It seems a city of
passage. People are running from something like animals
from a fire. Bill looks behind her. Her mother drags her
feet heavily in protest. She is staring into a shop window.
Something has caught her eye. She is looking at a hat.
"Pet, do look at this," she says, panting and pointing to
a red velvet hat with a green feather. Bill looks behind
them and thinks she sees the glint of silver hair, the
cherub cheeks, the rotund form, the small feet in the shiny
shoes. She hears the sharp, short tap of the shoes. She
grasps her mother's hand.

The girls at school join hands around the new girl from
England. They form a circle and chant under the loquat

tree. The new girl is plump and pasty-faced and has a limp white plait. The mosquitoes have bitten her, and there are big red welts all over her white flesh.

The new girl clips her words strangely. She says *drawing room* and *sand shoes* instead of *lounge* and *tackies*. When she listens to opera on the gramophone, Bill giggles.

The girl stands trembling in the middle of the circle, spitting on the mosquito bites on her pasty arm. Bill calls the English girl a killer. Bill makes the other girls chant, "You killed Joan of Arc." Afterward Bill gives the girl the *black spot* to tell her she is marked for death.

Bill's mother says, "Like vultures, Pet. They pick at your bones like vultures."

John shakes his head and says, "The white man has failed us."

Someone comes up behind Bill and covers her eyes. Bill can smell the heavy perfume, feel the plump fingers fluttering on her eyelids, hear the deep breathing. She pulls the fingers away and turns around. The woman laughs, showing her big white teeth. She says, "There is no reason why we cannot be friends, you know."

Bill says, "Friends?"

The woman says, "I want you to think of me as a friend, as an older sister. I am not that old, you know; not too old to understand. Think of me as a confidante."

Bill asks, "What is it I must tell you?"

The woman sighs and purses her thick lips. "Why don't you tell me where you are going again this afternoon, where you always go in the afternoons, running around the streets, half-naked. You are worrying your mother to death, you know." Bill stares back into the yellow eyes.

Bill grasps her mother by the wrist, dragging her fast through the crowded street of the gold town. Like a small child her mother stumbles along, dragging on Bill's arm. Her dark hair falls across her eyes. She stops and closes her parasol, asking, "Why the hurry, Pet?"

"Just hurry," Bill says.

"But my head, Pet." The wind blows the gold dust about her head. The fine powder settles in her hair and on the narrow shoulders of her gray dress. She teeters. "The light gives me a headache," her mother says and shades her eyes with her hand.

Bill begs her father to keep the blue one for her. He pulls on his stiff mustache, smooths back his thick russet hair, and sighs. He looks up at the ceiling. He says, "I am already borrowing from Peter to pay Paul."

Her mother says that gold is another matter entirely, that the gold is very deep in the earth here, that you cannot just go out and hire yourself some Kaffirs and sit and read the *Rand Daily Mail* in the sun and have them bring it to you on a platter. You need machinery to mine gold. That is why most of the fools fail.

When the earth trembles, her mother shakes her head and mutters, "There they go, blasting in the mines again."

Uncle Charles never knows what has happened. He keeps saying, "Who would do such a thing?" He keeps on wailing when he finds the crushed bird, its head pressed against the bars of the cage.

The cactus grows in the rock garden like a green stone. The autumn light beats down like blades, carving the cactus to a sharp-edged stone, an emerald.

Bill watches the doctor and the woman in the white uniform emerge from her mother's room. The woman looks flushed, her lipstick smudged, her damp hair escaping from the sides of her white cap, her uniform rumpled. The doctor removes his hand from the woman's back when he sees Bill. "Your mother is sleeping now," he tells Bill gravely, and puts his hand on the jamb of the door. Bill walks toward the door.

"I wouldn't disturb your mother now, darling, if I were you," the woman in the white uniform says in her man's voice, blocking the door. She stands there solidly, with her bosom like a bolster, her legs apart, twin pillars. Bill thrusts past the woman, going through the door of the sickroom. The woman takes Bill by the shoulders and thrusts her out of the room, but not before Bill has seen her mother lying gray and still on the bed, and the flies buzzing around the sticky liquid that remains in her glass.

· · ·

She casts about and sees the poster on the wall. "Look," she says to her mother, pointing, "we'll go in there, and you can sit down and rest." Bill points to the entrance of the cinema, to the shadow of the marquee. "We can go in there and sit down out of the light."

Her mother looks up at the poster. She looks into the dark menacing eyes under the burnoose. She says, "You want me to go in there?"

"You can rest in there," Bill says.

Her mother gazes dumbly at the poster horseman. She sways back and forth. She clasps the end of her furled parasol, while the anonymous crowd moves around her in the hard light of the autumn afternoon.

Bill watches from the window on the staircase as the woman arrives, stepping down from the victoria, one, two, in the white uniform that is increasingly too tight in the right places. She enters the hallway with the doctor, stopping before the mirror to adjust the cap that lists slightly like a boat on the sea of her wavy gold hair. She smiles at the doctor. Bill can see her pink tongue.

The doctor whistles a little tune and pulls on his waist-coat. He leans toward her, and she murmurs something. The doctor laughs, and they sail up the steps together, coming on relentlessly toward Bill.

They do what she wants them to do. They murmur to her, and then they do what she wants. They sit beside her on the bench by the lake in the green shade and tell her she has lovely hair, bright hazel eyes, or that she has a special languorous glow, or other things she does not hear. She hardly listens, hardly sees their gray faces. She watches the ducks on the lake dipping their glittering green heads. She watches the weeds growing in the water. She watches the afternoon dissolve. She thinks of the horseman riding across desert sand.

Sometimes she winds her fingers through her hair and says, "You may touch it if you like, but that would be extra." One of them, she remembers, touches her hair very gently with clean dry hands that have that dark scent under the scent of soap like the doctor's.

Bill looks behind, but there is no one following. There is no shadow behind her. She cannot see her mother. Her mother has let go of Bill's hand in the crowd. Bill stands on the curb, peering into the crowd. She cannot see her mother in the crush of people. Her mother has slipped away from her. Something has snatched her mother up. The crowd has swallowed her up. The cars stop honking. The crowd seems quiet. Bill hears a sudden stillness in the street.

The gold is in the sky, the smoke floats in the air, the dust lingers, but her mother has vanished. A flag flaps, whips, and unfurls with the sound of a beating sail. Bill's tunic flaps, whips around her legs. She looks across the street, but she sees no sign of her mother. It is as if a boat has pulled away from the shore in the night—floating on a sea of people. There is nothing in Bill's eyes but darkness.

Then she sees her mother standing in the shadows on the other side of the street. Her mother has been swept across the street with the crowd. She looks very far off, as small as a moth hovering beneath the light of the giant eyes of the horseman. She is leaning against the wall in her gray chiffon dress. She is in the shadows under the marquee. Drawing nearer to her, Bill is sure, is the doctor. Like a bandit, the doctor will be onto her mother now.

At dinner, the woman wears a stiff, shiny dress that matches her eyes. Sparks fly from the gold dress as she moves. Sparks burn Bill as the woman brushes her plump hand playfully on the back of Bill's neck as she goes by her chair. The woman sits in the chair beside Bill's father in her stiff, shiny dress and flashes her feverish eyes across the dinner table. She sits there wetting her lips in the dry air. She lights a cigarette and the smoke coils and lingers on Bill's father's face. He stares before him blankly and pushes his food across his plate. His square shoulders press against the chair in his fine tweed jacket. His eyes are a cool ash-gray. Something kindles in his eyes, flickers, Bill sees, and he crushes his napkin in his hand, lays it down by his plate. Bill drops her knife to the floor and bends down under the table and stares into the dim light.

. . .

Bill comes in from the light and lies on her bed in the darkness of the shuttered room. She waits for the angel to appear at the end between the bars in a luminous cloud, to spread wide the rainbow-colored wings and sing her to sleep. She waits for the angel to lie close to her, with the halo around the head, the luminous face, to see her without eyes and sing to her without a mouth and to touch her without hands.

Bill stares at the sunlight piercing the blades of the blinds. The sunlight makes her boots look cut up, makes Dottie's dark hair on her upper lip darker, makes the wide mouth grimace.

Bill waits for Dottie to speak to her father, but she stands in silence, her mouth open, her gloved hands clenched. Her father stares at Dottie patiently. "What is it, my dear?" he asks blankly.

Bill says, "I'll tell you."

Her father looks at Bill and says, "Let your elder sister speak first."

Bill urges, "Well, go ahead, Dottie, for goodness sake, tell him."

There is a painting done in pastels in the lounge above the fireplace. A half-dressed woman is bending over to adjust a blue slipper. The strap of her negligee has fallen down her arm, and her collarbone and small breasts are visible. She turns her head and looks toward the door. A man's head appears, thrust mysteriously through the half-opened door.

What Dottie says, finally, is, "I think she has gone mad!" and weeps dramatically. Bill watches the flowers in Dottie's hat shake ridiculously and thinks Dottie is overdoing it a bit, enjoying the drama.

The father shifts his inexpressive eyes, moves something across his desk with a sad gesture. He says, "Now, now, pull yourself together. No need for the waterworks, Dorothy." He presses a coin into Bill's hand and says, "Now, you two run along and buy yourselves some cake and some strawberry ice cream."

On the dusty stairs, Bill says to Dottie, "Fat lot of good that did."

Bill wakes and sits up straight in her bed as though shaken awake by a hand. She sees a beam of moonlight shining on the nursery floor. She opens the door and slips along the lit hallway and stands before the door of the small room where the woman sleeps. The door is ajar, the room lit by the light of the moon. The great still moon makes the room amazingly visible. There is the empty bed with the covers drawn back. There is the dresser with the cigarette burns, the cracked mirror. Bill opens the drawers of the dresser quietly and takes out the knitting needles from the bottom drawer. She listens to the sound of soft breathing. She sees the curtain move and the woman step out from behind it. Bill can see her gold hair, her flashing eyes, the dark folds of her robe.

The woman stands motionless in the middle of the room, as if fascinated, staring at the knitting needles in Bill's hand. She says quickly, "You want me to show you a secret?" Bill holds the knitting needles tightly in her hand.

The woman says, "This is something you will not see anywhere else." Bill says nothing but does not move away. The woman laughs and lifts her chin to one side. Slowly, she turns, lowers her head, and raises the dark robe. Her plump leg glistens in the moonlight, and Bill sees something blue. She draws nearer. The woman bends her knee outward, twists her leg, and shows Bill the inside of her thick thigh. Bill sees the small tattooed butterflies, winging their way up the white of the woman's thigh.

The woman looks at Bill's face and laughs. "See, I told you you would like it," she says. She reaches out, takes the knitting needles from Bill's hand. For a moment, she resists. Then the woman places the tip of Bill's index finger against the thigh. The woman traces the wing of a butterfly near the knee with Bill's finger. Breathless, Bill watches the woman fly her finger from wing to wing, soaring along the thigh to the butterfly at the summit.

Bill is trying to make her way across the crowded street. She hears the sound of the stamp and shuffle of feet. She sees the women swaying their hips; she sees the glossy lips, the brightness of their eyes. She sees the dark eyes of the horseman that stare down at them through the dusty air.

Then the sun is in Bill's eyes, and she blinks. She thinks she catches sight of the doctor approaching her mother with his silver hair, his plump fingers. The shadows flick on his short legs. He is onto her mother now. Bill will not allow it. She will not let it happen.

People stand in doorways, staring, as Bill plunges recklessly through the traffic. An elderly lady in black peers through a lorgnette as Bill grasps her mother's wrist and drags her forward into the shadow of the marquee. They disappear into the cinema, out of the light.

One of them follows her down R. Street. Their shadows meet and mingle on the pavement. In the chill light of the autumn dusk, the grass on the pavement has a yellowish pall. She turns to him and asks what he wants. He lights a cigarette in the shadow of a tree and asks her if she believes in fate.

"Fate?" she asks.

He says, "You know, chance meetings, like Beatrice and Dante." She tilts her head to one side. She stands there facing him, turning her copper bracelets around her wrist. She draws nearer and gives him a kiss.

"You do that very well." he says, blinking.

She leaves a note in the older girl's plastic mug, propped up beside the toothbrush and the toothpaste on the shelf with all the other mugs in the bathroom at school. She takes the girl into her bed after lights-out and holds her like a lover. Her body is soft and white.

When they lay the girl out in the dry grass, her face is gray and her small chin is tipped up toward Bill, as though she is showing Bill that she is dead.

While the one with the greasy hair has his hands around her neck, he talks about God. All the time he holds her pushed up against the willow tree, he mumbles something about God the Father, God the Son, and God the Holy Ghost. He is doing something to himself down there and talking about God. She sees something white glimmer while he touches himself and talks about the Holy Ghost. She thinks she is going to die. They will find her body floating in the water with the weeds.

Afterward, her mother touches Bill's neck with her shaking hands. Her mother tells Bill to cover her neck so that no one will see.

Afterward, what Bill remembers is the clear oval of her mother's lit face, the shimmer of her hair, the parched lips parted, the abject gaze, the way she murmurs, "Lovely, lovely, I will never see anything as lovely again."

She hears the sound of the piano as she stands in the half dark of the lobby of the cinema and buys two tickets fast. Her mother stands beside her, shifting from foot to foot. She says, "Not in there, Pet, please."

Bill says, "No one will find us in there."

Her mother says, "My head, Pet, my head."

Bill says, "You will see, it's lovely in there."

Bill grasps her mother by the wrist and pulls her forward. Her mother stumbles blindly in the sudden dark. Bill is half dragging her mother, half carrying her into fitful light. They are making their way into the desert light with the sound of the woman playing the piano. Her mother is slipping from Bill's grasp, sinking down into her seat, her head falling backward with a little moan. She is sitting in a seat in the half dark at the back of the cinema, panting. The light flickers on her face. She seems to doze off quickly. She hardly moves. Bill can see the white light flickering on her mother's cheek. Bill sees the powder on her mother's cheek like dust. Then her mother opens her eyes, stares at the screen. Bill sits down beside her mother and stares at the screen. Together, they watch the horseman riding across the desert sand.

Bill stands at the door to the sickroom and watches the doctor rise from her mother's bed. Bill watches the woman in the white uniform lean toward him, letting her cheek brush against his legs, letting the folds of her thin uniform stretch and part as she moves. The doctor whispers something in her ear. The woman leans over Bill's mother on the bed. The woman takes the mother's hand, caresses her arm, her neck, her shoulders. The woman's hands descend toward the mother's breasts. The woman rubs and soothes, calls the mother dearie, and props her head against her own starched, heavy bosom. The woman holds the glass to the mother's parted lips.

She does not need to open her eyes. She sees without having to see. She sits there, her eyes hard, as though lidless, stone. She watches in the night of her mind and listens to the woman who is playing on the piano the accompaniment to her dreams. Bill invents the desert, the palms, the white light. She makes the sun shine. She makes the people move across the landscape under killing light. She makes the horseman strut in his boots, his hand on his hip, his teeth gleaming, his eyes flashing. The woman throws back her head and parts her lips and lifts her abject gaze. The light shines in her hair. The woman's dagger glints as she drives it through her own heart.

Bill knows that the people in the cinema are staring at them and whispering as they turn in their seats. She holds them, too, in the palm of her hand. She turns to her mother and watches her stare blankly at the screen, the screen of Bill's mind.

The wind moans. The mutilated branches of the trees lift toward the sky. The door rattles. The transparent curtains lift and fall. Flies buzz about the sticky liquid left in the glass beside the bed.

Her mother sleeps on her side, one arm stretched above her head. Her fingers clutch the bars as though she seeks to impede her fall. She floats in her thin silk gown like an odalisque. The light glows around her head like a crown.

Bill touches her mother's arm and runs her hand down her damp back. She rolls her mother over onto her back and opens the gown. Bill touches the breasts, the buttocks, the thighs. She feels the film of sweat like milk. She bends over to smell her mother's thighs, the acrid scent between them. She touches the thighs with her tongue, licks at them, laps at the milky skin.

The paintings, the fans, the china Buddha on the dressing table, the heart-shaped pincushion flicker in the blue light.

Her mother stirs in her seat in the cinema, rolls her head back, and swings her loose hair with a supple movement, brushing her shoulders lightly in the dream-light of the film. She parts her lips, and Bill can smell her sweet, child's breath.

Bill takes her mother's hand, and runs her fingers over the rings and the narrow wrist.

Her mother says, "Lovely, lovely," as she weeps in fits and starts, "I will never again see anything as lovely."

Bill rises and makes her way into the corridor. She sees something in the corridor outside the sickroom in the dawn light. In the rosy glow of first light from the window, she sees two figures facing one another in dead silence. It is the dead silence and the intensity of the gaze that makes Bill step back. For a moment, she thinks she sees the doctor standing there motionless, facing the woman who gazes at him fixedly in her dark gown. Then she sees the russet hair, the stiff mustache, the pale eyes.

Bill slips the brown paper packet into her mother's lap. Her mother unties the string with trembling fingers, lifts up the locket with the photograph, the gold cigarette case, Dottie's garnet cross, the diamond ring, the coins from the *tickie* bottle. Bill lets the coins fall into her mother's lap, along with the brooches, the watch with the inscription to someone else's wife, the rings, the locket in the shape of a heart, the photograph of someone unknown, and the razor.

Her mother sifts through the jewels and lifts them up into the half-light. She picks up the razor, the one Bill stole from her father's medicine chest, and looks at Bill inquiringly.

Bill rises in the half-dark and looks down at her mother, who is trembling. The film goes on, beautiful. Bill turns her back on her mother, on the film. She sees only darkness as she walks down the aisle in silence.

She runs along the road toward the sun. The wind is at her back. She runs toward the house on the other side of town. The wind blows in gusts, a dry wind. Gray birds rise a little way in the air when the wind blows. When the wind dies, they descend and perch precariously on their thin legs in the red dust. She can see their glittering eyes.

When she comes back to the house on R. Street, she stumbles through the garden gate. The sun is low, the sky a dead yellow. The garden seems blanched; all the colors sucked by the sun. The trees spread skeleton arms against the sky. The plants wilt in the haze. Only the stiff cactus and the red-hot pokers remain upright. Their fleshy leaves shine in the sun as she runs along the dusty driveway, the wind on her back, the palm leaves swaying raggedly. Beds of bright daisies bend and sway beside the weed-choked grass. A rare bloom remains here and there.

She rings the front doorbell. The house shakes and recovers. When no one answers, she attempts to enter by the dining room doors, but she finds them locked. She rings the bell to a side entrance, a sunken door, buried by creeper, a servant's entrance. The harsh, sudden clang of the bell in the garden's stillness makes her start. Finally, the servant emerges.

He opens the door slowly with a creak of loose hinges and stands there blinking in the sunlight. He mutters something unintelligible and shuffles blindly across the lawn. She enters the shuttered house, makes her way alone through the dark passageway and up a flight of stairs into the pantries. The sound of her steps on the white stone floor echoes in the profound silence of the sleeping house.

In the dim light of the kitchen, she drinks a glass of cool water. She walks through the hall, with its bowl of dusty proteas and the shell-shaped cups and saucers locked in the china cabinet.

The hall is as cool as a vault. She goes up the carpeted stairs and into the nursery, where she stands staring at the brass beds gleaming in a ray of light that penetrates a chink in the curtains. She watches her sisters sleep in the afternoon light. Dottie lies on her back, her mouth open, her big hands folded as if in prayer on her chest. Haze's sheet has fallen onto the ground, and her pink knees are drawn up to her chest.

She goes through the shuttered rooms of the sleeping house in the half dark without letting a hand brush the velvet back of a chair. She makes her way along by memory through the spiderweb of darkened corridors. She catches a glimpse of herself in the standing mirror by the door of the sickroom, notices when she faces the mirror that her nose has a slight curve.

She enters and looks about her. She stares at the shimmer of yellow light lapping at the end of the bed. The room is redolent of perfume, something dark and succulent. In the pale light, she perceives the strange pictures, the glinting glass, the feathered fans, the thickly clustering plants.

She sees the clothes strewn on the armchair, the stockings hanging limply over the edge of the chair by their suspenders, the rumpled bed. The sheets are turned back, and the mosquito net coiled at the head. There is a white enamel pitcher, chipped at the rim, in a basin on the table by the bed. Bill stares at the bed, the brass bars, the silk gown arranged on the pillows, pulled in at the waist as though there were someone inside, as though someone had been laid out limply on the bed.

She moves across the room. Her hands hover like moths over the clutter on the dressing table: the silver-topped bottles, the jars, the silver-framed photographs, the cut-glass bowl, the Buddha, his stomach protruding from his gold robe. She touches the naked belly of the Buddha. He rocks slowly back and forth on the glass. Her hands look like someone else's hands, her mother's hands, the skin spotted like the skin of a snake.

A long time before, she crawled beneath the dark mauve skirts of this dressing table, looked up through the folds to watch her mother pull the hot wax from her upper lip with a short, sharp snap of the wrist.

She tiptoes into Uncle Charles's room. While Uncle Charles snores and sweats on his leather sofa in the dim afternoon light, Bill opens the doors of the cages and lets the birds fly free. They fly out the window. They rise in the air, flutter into the light, and settle in the fig tree. They fly tentatively, as though trying out an element no longer familiar. Their wings batter and blunder. The brightly colored birds flit from branch to branch cau-

tiously. Their muted cries splinter the silence. Then they
are aloft again. They disappear into white light like dust.

Her father shouts, "She couldn't have disappeared off the
face of the earth!"

The policeman mumbles, "People do disappear, I am
afraid. Perhaps she has gone on a voyage of some sort."

She walks fast down the driveway in the harsh light to
take the victoria to the hairdresser on her own. She sits
there, shivering, in the glare of light, with the stiff white
towel wrapped tightly around her neck and her shoulders
like a shroud. She hears the snip of the scissors. She feels
the cold of the steel on her neck. She tells the hairdresser,
a woman with long green nails and glossy butterfly lips,
to cut it shorter at the nape of the neck. She says,
"Shorter, I want it as short as it can get at the back." She
asks the woman to shave the hair at the back of her neck
and leave the sides long. She has seen someone who
looks like this in a film.

She looks at herself in the mirror, at the short hair,
released from the weight of its length, curling around her
face. Her face looks fuller, the cheeks whiter; the forehead
higher, the sweat visible around the brow; her mouth
looks darker, the lips thicker, a sensuous curve; the teeth
flash and the eyes shimmer darkly.

The cut hair lies about her on the floor in shining coils,
like the discarded skin of a snake.

. . .

It is so long, she can sit on it. Every night, she brushes it a hundred times, but when she cuts it off, she does so without a word to anyone. She takes a victoria into town on her own and has it done.

When her father questions her, Bill lies on the bed in the sickroom with a handkerchief on her face. She complains of the migraine and of fatigue. Her father stands at the foot of the bed, his hands clasping the brass bars and shouts, "Are you listening to me? Take that fool thing off your face!" Bill removes the handkerchief, sits up, and smiles at him.

Her father sits down heavily on the edge of the bed. The springs of the bed groan. He puts his head in his hands and weeps. He says, "What is to be done?"

She tells him that perhaps her mother will come back one day, the way the Zulu did, stumbling up the driveway with a brown paper packet in his hands. She tells her father that all she, Bill, wanted was to see the horseman sweep across desert sands.

At mealtimes they sit beside one another at the mahogany table with the feet like animals' claws. For months he refuses to say a word to her. He sits there, slightly stooped, his face the color of brick. He stares at the starched white tablecloth. He wipes his stiff mustache with his napkin.

She sees him smoke his thin cigar in silence.

A NOTE ABOUT THE AUTHOR

Sheila Kohler was born in South Africa and schooled in France and Switzerland. She holds an advanced degree from Columbia University and is the author of *Miracles in America* and *The Perfect Place*. She lives in New York City.

A NOTE ON THE TYPE

This book was set on the Monotype in Fournier, a
type face named for Pierre Simon Fournier, a
celebrated type designer in eighteenth-century
France. Fournier's type is considered transitional in
that it drew its inspiration from the old style yet
was ingeniously innovational, providing for an
elegant yet legible appearance. For some time after
his death in 1768, Fournier was remembered
primarily as the author of a famous manual of
typography and as a pioneer of the point system.
However, in 1925, his reputation was enhanced
when the Monotype Corporation of London
revived Fournier's roman and italic.

Composed by Crane Typesetting Service, Inc.,
West Barnstable, Massachusetts
Printed and bound by The Haddon Craftsmen,
Scranton, Pennsylvania
Designed by Virginia Tan